PUFFIN BOOKS

MUMMY MADNESS

Picture the scene: I'm at the RSPCA, choosing a dog.

'And what kind of dog are you looking for, sir?'

My eyes are shining. 'A secret agent,' I say, grinning with excitement. 'A dog that's capable of defeating evil baddies. One that can drive a car and surf the web. And it needs to be pretty useful in hand-to-hand combat, maybe a black belt,' I say, demonstrating by punching the air. 'Needs to look cool in shades too.'

The RSPCA lady mouths something under her breath which I don't quite catch. She thinks for a while before flashing me a polite smile. 'We're all out of those, sir. How about this one?' She points to a black and white mongrel whose sad face shows no sign of intelligence and who couldn't fight its way out of a wet paper bag. 'She's called Lara. Interesting ears.'

My heart sinks. 'OK,' I sigh. 'I'll use my imagination.'

Books by Andrew Cope

Spy Dog
Spy Dog Captured!
Spy Dog Unleashed!
Spy Dog Superbrain
Spy Dog Rocket Rider
Spy Dog Secret Santa
Spy Dog Teacher's Pet
Spy Dog Rollercoaster!
Spy Dog Brainwashed
Spy Dog Mummy Madness

Spy Pups Treasure Quest
Spy Pups Prison Break
Spy Pups Circus Act
Spy Pups Danger Island
Spy Pups Survival Camp

Spy Cat Summer Shocker

Spy Dog Joke Book

SPY DOG
Mummy Madness

ANDREW COPE

Illustrated by James de la Rue

PUFFIN

PUFFIN BOOKS

Published by the Penguin Group

Penguin Books Ltd, 80 Strand, London WC2R ORL, England

Penguin Group (USA) Inc., 375 Hudson Street, New York, New York 10014, USA

Penguin Group (Canada), 90 Eglinton Avenue East, Suite 700, Toronto, Ontario, Canada M4P 2Y3
(a division of Pearson Penguin Canada Inc.)

Penguin Ireland, 25 St Stephen's Green, Dublin 2, Ireland (a division of Penguin Books Ltd)

Penguin Group (Australia), 707 Collins Street, Melbourne, Victoria 3008, Australia
(a division of Pearson Australia Group Pty Ltd)

Penguin Books India Pvt Ltd, 11 Community Centre, Panchsheel Park, New Delhi – 110 017, India

Penguin Group (NZ), 67 Apollo Drive, Rosedale, Auckland 0632, New Zealand
(a division of Pearson New Zealand Ltd)

Penguin Books (South Africa) (Pty) Ltd, Block D, Rosebank Office Park, 181 Jan Smuts Avenue,
Parktown North, Gauteng 2193, South Africa

Penguin Books Ltd, Registered Offices: 80 Strand, London WC2R ORL, England

puffinbooks.com

First published 2014
002

Text copyright © Andrew Cope, 2014
Illustrations copyright © James de la Rue, 2014
All rights reserved

The moral right of the author and illustrator has been asserted

Set in Bembo Book MT Std 15/18 pt
Typeset by Palimpsest Book Production Limited, Falkirk, Stirlingshire
Printed in Great Britain by Clays Ltd, St Ives plc

British Library Cataloguing in Publication Data
A CIP catalogue record for this book is available from the British Library

ISBN: 978-0-141-34431-7

www.greenpenguin.co.uk

MIX
Paper from
responsible sources
FSC
www.fsc.org   FSC® C018179

Penguin Books is committed to a sustainable
future for our business, our readers and our planet.
This book is made from Forest Stewardship
Council™ certified paper.

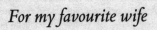

For my favourite wife

Contents

Contents

1. HAPI Days

The children loved it when Professor Cortex came over to their house. But it was even more special when they visited him in his secret laboratory.

Lara, her puppies and the children sat in the reception area, sipping their milkshakes. The professor had issued instructions that they were to try his newly invented flavours while they waited. Ben and Sophie were sucking up mouthfuls of 'bread & butter' flavour. Ollie was noisily hoovering up the last of his 'tea & biscuit'. All three dogs had gone for 'fish 'n' chip' milkshakes, with Spud eyeing up 'bangers & mash' to try next.

'Not bad,' woofed Lara to the pups. 'And an interesting break with tradition to have savoury milkshakes. Perfect for pets. I can see these flying off the supermarket shelves!'

If there was a competition for the 'cleverest person on the planet', Professor Maximus Cortex would be the outright winner. He was in charge of the government's top-secret Spy School and spent a great deal of his time doing whacky research. He'd come to love Ben, Sophie and Ollie over the years. They'd provided a home for his greatest-ever achievement. And here she was, tail swishing and a silly doggie grin spread across her face.

'GM451,' beamed the professor, swooping through the door. 'Good to see you again. And Agents Star and Spud. I trust you're keeping the town clear of crime?'

Reported crime down 68 per cent, thought Lara. *Burglaries down 80 per cent. No reported shoplifting and last quarter's mugging statistics were zero.*

'We need to get my finest canine agents up to speed with the latest inventions. You can never be too careful,' he said, tapping the side of his nose and spooking the children. 'Enemies are everywhere,' he said, eyebrow raised, eyes darting left and right.

Ollie, the youngest of the three, followed the

professor's eyes, looking round the room for suspicious people. 'I don't think there are any baddies in here,' he smiled. 'Just me and my brother and sister. And our doggies.'

'And can you stop calling Lara "GM451"?' nagged Sophie. 'She's not a spy any more, Professor. She's retired, OK? And she's our family pet. And, even more importantly, she's got pups of her own.'

Nice one, Soph, thought Lara. *It's always good to remind the mad prof that his first-ever 'Licensed Assault and Rescue Animal', LARA, is officially an ex-Spy Dog. No need for code names any more.*

'Old habits and all that,' flustered the professor. 'GM451 might have retired, but her enemies most certainly haven't. Which is why we need to keep you all up to speed.'

Spud had spied an open packet of digestive biscuits in the professor's pocket. *I'd like to be kept up to speed with those*, he thought, his tail swishing in excitement. In Spud's world gadgets were cool, but food was always his top priority. Spud's motto was that a canine agent operates best on a full tummy. 'You never know where your next meal's coming from,' he explained to his sister. 'So I'm always on full alert. For food!'

Star was more of an all-action hero. While her brother had a roly-poly puppy look about him, she was slimline and fit. Her black and white fur shone and her eyes glistened. Star listened intently as the white-coated professor went about his business.

'Right, follow me, team, I have something exciting to show you,' he said.

The dogs and children hurried along behind the scientist. They trotted behind his billowing coat as he marched down endless white corridors. The professor stopped abruptly at a door that was being guarded by a burly man dressed in black.

'Cool shades,' whispered Ben out of the side of his mouth. 'But why's he wearing them indoors?'

'Agent T,' said the professor, 'I'd like to introduce you to our visitors. Would you please open the door and accompany us into the top-secret laboratory?'

Agent T pressed some numbers on a control pad and the door slid open. The small troop entered the lab and the door swished shut, Agent T guarding the exit.

Cooool, thought Lara, scanning the room,

taking in the bubbling potions and whiteboards full of equations. *I'm glad he's on our side! I shudder to think what would happen if the professor's brainpower fell into the wrong hands.*

'Inventions,' grinned the professor, sweeping his hand round the room. 'This is where ideas get transferred from here,' he said, jabbing a finger at his head, 'to here,' he said, holding up a test tube of purple liquid. 'How did you get on with my new milkshakes?'

'Yummy,' grinned Ollie.

'Excellent,' beamed the professor. 'This one's in development.' He pointed at a formula scribbled on the board. 'Frogs' legs flavour,' he said. 'It has a very interesting taste. But I'm also thinking of crisps,' he added, peering over the top of his spectacles. 'Gap in the market, you see. Nobody's doing frogs' legs crisps.'

Spud's ears stood to attention. *Cool idea, Prof!*

Sophie shuddered. 'I think you'll find there's a reason for that, Professor,' she said, crinkling her nose up at the idea. 'Frogs' legs are yukky!'

'Yes, yes,' tutted the professor as if the idea had never crossed his mind. 'Maybe we'll aim it at the, erm, *continental* market?'

'What's that formula over there?' asked Ben, pointing at a sequence of letters and shapes that took up an entire wall.

'That one's not exactly new,' the professor mused, 'more a development of an earlier prototype.' He pointed to a Bunsen burner heating a bottle of the purple liquid. 'I distil this little brew,' he smiled, 'into these marvellous crystals.' He held up a small jar. 'And, I have to tell you, this is the most fun you can have in a secret laboratory.'

Ben looked confused. 'What's fun about a few crystals?'

'These little beauties,' said the professor, holding up the jar so everyone could see, 'will bring humour to any situation.'

'I don't get it,' chirped Sophie.

'Well,' mused the scientist, 'you've probably heard of laughing gas. It's all rather complex, but, to cut a long story very short, I've worked out that it's the interconnectedness of the amygdala and hypothalamus that allows the prefrontal part of the hippocampus to create meta-programmes that accentuate the . . .'

Professor Cortex stopped and observed the children's glazed eyes. 'I'm doing it again, aren't I?' he smiled.

'Ollie's six, Prof,' said Ben. 'Keep it simple.'

'Quite,' nodded the scientist, pushing his spectacles back up his nose. 'I've analysed the part of the brain that creates laughter,' he continued. 'And these crystals scramble the emotional part of the brain to convert all emotions to "hilarious". So the person experiences an acute sense of humour. Anything and everything is funny. And I'm not talking "mildly amusing", I'm talking "side-splittingly hilarious". I call them HAPI crystals. Hyper Acute Positive Intervention,' coughed the professor, beaming over the top of his spectacles. 'Do you see what I did there? I took the H from Hyper and the A from . . .'

'We get it, Prof,' interrupted Ben. 'HAPI. Very good.'

'Everything?' asked Ollie. 'You said *everything* is funny.'

'Absolutely,' assured the professor. 'All you have to do is drop a few crystals on the floor and grind them in with your foot. They release gas, you see, which seeps into your nervous system to create laughter. And not just a small chuckle. We're talking laughter until it hurts. Agent T had to attend a funeral last week and we tested the capsules under extremely sad conditions.'

Agent T nodded, recalling the hilarity of the church service.

'The vicar laughed so much he pulled a muscle in his stomach. Isn't that right, Agent T?'

'Affirmative, sir,' nodded the man from behind his dark glasses. 'And one of the family was laughing so hard that they fell into the grave, sir,' he reminded the professor. 'It's on YouTube, sir.'

'Indeed it is,' nodded the professor. 'And you wet yourself, Agent T. During the vicar's speech. Isn't that correct?'

The man in the dark suit twitched as he recalled the embarrassment.

'It's great at disabling baddies,' explained the scientist. 'But I see a big commercial market for it. I might have to reduce the strength of the formula to give it more mass appeal,' he thought aloud. 'But everyone wants to be happier, right? And laughing is good for you. So why not introduce more laughter into your life?'

'But,' noted Sophie, 'aren't funerals supposed to be sad? Isn't that the point? Is it appropriate to chuckle your way through such a serious and important occasion?'

'Details, details,' dismissed the professor, swishing his hand at Sophie. 'I'll work it out after we've experimented. In the meantime,

Benjamin, take this packet of crystals and use them wisely.' He handed Ben a small package. 'Emergencies only,' he winked. 'Because, after all, you never know when adventure will strike.'

2. The Legend of the Nile Ruby

Egypt, July 1953

The sun was relentless and their rations were low. A dashing young man removed his sweat-stained hat and mopped his forehead. He consulted the old map one last time. It was yellowed and crinkled but still legible. His finger traced the route they'd taken. The dotted line showed they'd trekked 103 miles west of the Egyptian capital. The pyramids had been left far behind.

'Everyone's looking there,' he reminded his father. 'A seething mass of tourism and tomb robbers.'

His father's eyes sparkled with excitement. He squinted at the map and nodded. Before they'd set off from Cairo, they'd heard that yet another part of the Great Pyramid had been raided. 'They've taken everything,' he muttered. 'The looters are destroying ancient history. The pharaohs knew. That's why they made the pyramids so big. The may as well have put a sign, with a huge arrow, saying: "Jewels buried here. Break in and help yourselves."'

The men pored over the map one last time. 'Not far now,' said the younger of the two, pointing to the picture of caves on the map. 'The final resting place of Pharaoh Qua'a and the *real* Egyptian treasure.'

The older man grinned, his blackened teeth showing through his bushy beard. He'd spent fifty years exploring Egyptian tombs with no reward. And then he'd discovered this map and the black book that came with it. He and his son were the only two people on the planet to know the secret of the ancients – that the pyramids were a big, fat decoy. The pharaohs built huge pyramids to attract thieves. But all they really held were worthless treasures that would throw the tomb robbers off the scent.

The biggest and most precious of all Egyptian treasures was actually buried 103 miles away. Great care had been taken to hide the Nile Ruby in the most unmemorable place imaginable.

Who would ever think of looking for the world's
most precious gem in a tunnel at the back of a
cave? One hundred miles of sand and rock in

every direction. Even if people found the cave, the ancients had gone to great trouble to make sure that the tunnel would never be discovered.

And when the pharaoh died there was a grand ceremony in Cairo and a body was hidden in the Great Pyramid. But, as the father and son now knew, it was *a* body. Not *the* body. Nobody had ever found Qua'a. 'Because,' as the old man explained, 'the body had been secretly taken from Cairo and hauled by camel to the caves. Only one man knew. The trusted servant, who was to die with the pharaoh, sealing himself in from inside the tunnel. And the skeleton of that loyal servant will still be there, guarding his master.'

The servant's only son had inherited the map. He could neither read nor write and the map passed down through the generations until it found itself on sale in a Cairo market.

'Three thousand years later and here we are,' announced the old man, pointing at the heap of grey rocks standing out in the yellow sand. A sandstorm was whipping up around them. He licked a finger and flipped a page in the book. 'Exactly as described,' he yelled through the gathering storm.

He and his son staggered into the cave, delighted to be out of the stinging sand. It was eerily quiet. The old man took a handkerchief from his pocket and blew out a noseful of sand. The younger man struck a long match and cupped the light in his hand. His father pulled a candle from his backpack and the cave was lit

with an eerie glow. Shadows danced on the cave ceiling. The men made their way to the back of the cave and the young man stretched his arm towards the wall. 'What is it I'm looking for again?'

His father tapped the black book. 'Man with dog's head,' he reminded his son. 'Qua'a's sign.'

The young man swished the candle across the back of the cave. 'Nothing,' he said, looking disappointed. 'Wait!' he yelled. 'What's this?' He rubbed the cave wall with his sleeve and drew the candle nearer. He turned to his father. 'Man with dog's head! The legend is true. Qua'a was here!'

3. Crazy Dez

Hurtmore was what all high-security prisons should be: tall, grey and serious. There had been several escape attempts, but only one success. And even that hadn't lasted long: Mr Big was back inside again and security had been upped from 'maximum' to 'ultra'. The old prison chief had been replaced, as had Mr Big's bars. Spy Dog had been consulted when they designed the ultra-security features. After all, she was the agent who was most familiar with the workings of Mr Big's evil mind. The bars were now twice as thick and electric fences had been erected in front of and behind the twenty-metre-high walls. There were huge spikes on top, just to make sure. As the prison chief had explained when Big had been recaptured, 'Nothing's too much trouble for you, Big.'

The world's nastiest criminal shared a cell with an old man. The prison governor had been very careful whom to select. Most of the officers considered the old man to be mad. He was frail so would do Big no harm and, it was hoped, Big would see no reason to hurt him either. And, in a strange code of conduct, the prison boss had realized that the world's most evil criminal did observe one rule. He respected his elders.

So the odd couple shared a cell. Big would brag about his crimes and tell tales of a nutty professor, some meddling kids and a dratted dog. 'Lost an eye, my teeth and a leg because of that dog. They had to rebuild me.' He looked around at the bars on his window. 'This place can't hold me,' he bragged. 'And when I'm out the dog will be no more. "Spy Dog" they call her. "Dead dog" more like.'

And, in return, the old man would babble about Egypt. And mummies. And Mr Big would listen politely to the white-haired old man, even if the story was the same every night. 'Yes, yes,' he'd sigh. 'The pyramids are a decoy. And you and your dad found the tomb . . . blah blah blah.'

'And can you keep a secret?' hissed the wizened old man, his eyes staring crazily. 'I've worked it out! The whole mystery is unravelled. The legend of the Nile Ruby! It's true! I know where it is.'

'Here you go again,' sighed Mr Big. 'It's written in the stars. You're a bit like a broken record. Now don't get me wrong, old boy, you're a nice fella and all that – remind me a bit of my own pa. He was a bit confused too. The Nile Ruby? Egypt?' Mr Big shook his head. 'Look around you. Check out the view from your window. It ain't Egypt out there. It's a maximum-security prison. And I hate to be the bearer of bad news, but the truth is that you're stuck in here till the day you die.'

Egypt, July 1953

The gale howled outside. The old man consulted his black book once more. 'Booby traps,' he hissed. 'Be very careful.' He pointed to a small rock set into the cave ceiling.

His son moved into position and handed the candle to his father. He reached up and pushed at the jutting rock. 'Nothing!'

'Push harder,' urged the old man. 'After three thousand years it's going to be stiff.'

The young man shifted position to get a better grip. He reached upwards and grabbed the rock. He grimaced as he heaved his shoulders upwards. The rock disappeared into the cave ceiling and there was a rumbling to their right. A small hole appeared. The old man was rejuvenated, almost skipping towards the hole. He reached his hand in and felt for the lever. He pulled. The back of the cave slid open, revealing a dark tunnel.

'Just as the book says,' he grinned.

They doubled their candle power. The younger man swigged the last of his water and they entered the tunnel.

They edged along, cupping the flames with one hand and feeling in the semi-darkness with the other. Eventually the passage widened out and they were relieved to be able to stand up. 'This must be Qua'a's cave,' gasped the old man, shining his candle at the parchment. He pressed his candle to a torch on the wall and a larger flame was lit. Both men gawped. They were in a much bigger cave. A large tomb took centre stage, the skeleton of Qua'a's servant sitting in a chair nearby. The cave was full of treasures. The flames reflected off golden goblets and silver headdresses. Gold coins were hanging from the ceiling, glinting like the night-time stars. All of Qua'a's worldly possessions had been stored here, in readiness for the afterlife.

The young man couldn't control his excitement. 'Just as it says in the book,' he yelled, his enthusiasm bouncing off the walls. 'Riches beyond anyone's wildest imagination! But the Nile Ruby, the biggest treasure of them all, is

in the tomb with Qua'a.' He rushed towards the tomb.

'No!' shouted his father, running after him. But it was too late. The young man's foot caught on the tripwire. He fell to the floor and the arrow fired over his head and thudded into his father. The young man crawled over and rolled him on to his back. The old man managed a smile and a nod. 'The Nile Ruby . . . my life's work is now your life's work,' he whispered with his last breath.

The young man wiped away a tear and a yell

of despair echoed round Qua'a's cave. His father had come so far and yet was not going to see his dream fulfilled. Qua'a's treasures had meant very little: the only thing that mattered was the Nile Ruby and now he would never get to see it. The young man looked down at his shaking hands and vowed that he would find the ruby and make sure the world knew that his father had solved the mystery. Everything in the book had been true. The pyramids were a clever trick. Qua'a, the richest and most powerful pharaoh, was buried right here in this long-lost tomb. And, according to the black book, the Nile Ruby was buried with him.

The skeleton appeared to be grinning. The young man edged round the cave, making sure there were no more wires. He carefully removed the grinning skeleton from its chair and sent his foot crashing through the seat. He chose the longest and strongest length of wood and slid it under the lid of the coffin. The young man heaved. The stone moved just a little and the skeleton guard seemed to grin even more. He wished his father could be there to help, but he somehow summoned the strength of two men and the lid of the tomb gradually slid to one side. He fell to his knees, his chest heaving, sweat pouring. He grabbed the candle and, bathed in golden light, he rose to his feet. He lowered the candle into the coffin and peered inside.

'Found you!' he gasped, his eyes focusing on the bandaged body of Qua'a. Time had blackened the bandages. His arms swept through the coffin, his eyes searching for the Nile Ruby. *Nothing!* He scrambled into the crypt and carefully lifted the mummified body out. *Still nothing.* 'It's an empty tomb!'

He looked at his father's body lying on the floor. 'The legend was wrong!' he yelled, tears streaming down his face. 'The pharaoh was buried *without* his most precious jewel.'

4. 'Titchology'

Ben knew his little brother was desperate to get his hands on the HAPI crystals so he took the packet and zipped it into his coat pocket out of the way.

'And that's not all,' grinned the professor. 'I have invented a, *ahem*, hand-held mobile phone,' he announced.

Lara raised a surprised doggie eyebrow and Sophie coughed, to stifle a laugh. 'Hand-held mobiles, Professor? I think you'll find they've been around for ages.'

Professor Cortex gave a disapproving glance and carried on. 'Not like this one, young lady,' he said, giving her his hardest stare. The professor held his right hand up and spread his fingers. 'You see the mobile is *in* the hand.'

Cool idea, thought Lara, her mind racing ahead.

Ollie looked at Ben. Ben looked at Ollie. They shrugged.

'This could be even worse than the daytime torch!' sighed Sophie, rolling her eyes.

The scientist pressed on, undaunted by the children's lack of enthusiasm. 'It's smaller than pico-technology, you see.'

'Pico?' repeated Ollie. 'Cool word.'

'Cool word indeed, young Oliver. Let me explain,' nodded the scientist, delighted to have an opportunity to share his knowledge. 'When I was growing up, and GM451 was just a pup, we had good old-fashioned "technology".'

Steady on, old boy, thought Lara. *I'm not that old!*

'And then things got smaller so we invented *micro*technology. And now most scientists are working on *nano*technology . . . which is smaller than micro.'

Ollie stifled a yawn.

'But they're light years behind. There is a Russian scientist who's working on *pico*-technology, which is so tiny that the human eye can't even see it.'

'Smaller than a flea?' asked Ollie, imagining the smallest thing he could.

Why's everyone looking at me? thought Lara, resisting the urge to scratch behind her ear.

'Smaller than a flea's brain cell,' nodded the professor. 'But, as usual, kiddiewinks, I'm ahead of the game. Fleas' brain cells are, quite frankly, far too big. We can do better. I'm working on technology so small that the human brain can't even *imagine* it. I've had to invent a new word for it. Forget "technology". I'm working on "*titch*ology".' The professor peered over the top of his spectacles to see what reaction there was to his new word. The children's faces were vacant. 'Titch,' he repeated, 'as in "titchy", which means "tiny". Can you see that I've replaced the "tech" bit with . . .'

'Nice one, Prof,' cut in Ben. 'We get it. To be honest, I'm more interested in seeing *titchology* in action. Have you got any gadgets?'

'Have I got any gadgets?' fussed the professor, flapping at the pockets in his white coat. 'Have I got any gadgets . . .' he repeated, looking a little flustered. 'The problem with titchology is that it's too small to see. Almost too titchy to imagine. So the gadgets sometimes, you know . . .' he continued, turning one of his jacket pockets inside out.

'Disappear?' suggested Sophie.

'Quite,' agreed the scientist. 'Benjamin, is your mobile switched on?'

'Yes, Professor,' said Ben, tapping his trouser pocket.

'Then let's try my device.' The children and dogs watched as the professor made his hand into the shape of a phone. 'Thumb up,' he explained, 'and little finger raised, like so.' He put his hand to his ear. 'It's like they do on TV talent contests when they want you to vote for them,' he explained. 'Not that I watch such rubbish. But I know that all those really annoying contestants make a hand signal like a phone. "*Vote for meee. Vote for meee!*" Except, you see, I have small implants under my skin so my hand *is* a phone.'

The professor waggled his thumb. 'Just getting a signal,' he explained. 'Zero seven six one one,' he began, talking to his little finger. 'Eight eight zero three five one.'

'That's my number,' said Ben, his eyes widening. Everyone jumped as Ben's ringtone rang out. He fumbled in his pocket and looked around at everyone.

'Well, go on then,' urged Sophie. 'Answer it. It might be Mum or someone.'

The professor chuckled as Ben slid open his phone and put it to his ear. 'Hello?' he began.

'Hello indeed,' said the professor into his little finger. 'Are you receiving, Benjamin? This is the professor calling from his revolutionary hand-held mobile device.'

Ben looked up. 'It's you!' he said, pointing at the professor. 'Talking from your . . . *hand phone*?'

'It most certainly is,' beamed the professor, turning and walking into the next room. 'So what do you think of my new invention?'

'It's kind of . . . weird,' stuttered Ben into his phone. 'And really cool, I suppose.'

'I agree,' came the professor's reply. 'One of my best-ever inventions. I mean, how many times have you lost your phone or had it stolen? You can't lose this one because it's implanted under the skin of your fingers.'

'Does it hurt?' asked Ben, talking into his mobile. 'I mean the implanting bit.'

'Not one jot,' assured the scientist. '"Titchology". Teeny-weeny. Unimaginably small. The question is, young man, would you want to buy one?'

'Of course,' stuttered Ben. 'It's the best invention ever.'

'Agreed again,' said the professor. 'As a famous astronaut sort of said, it's a small invention by me that will result in a huge leap for humankind. Or something like that. Anyway, over and out.' Professor Cortex shook his hand and the signal was lost. He bounded back into

30

the laboratory and stood hopping from foot to foot in what Sophie called the Mad Professor Dance.

The children's mouths were open. Ollie was jumping up and down with excitement. Spud was bounding round the room. 'That's the best thing ever, Prof,' he barked. 'Can you do one for dogs? I could have a hotline to the biscuit factory.'

Lara gave Spud a disapproving look.

'Humans only at this stage,' noted the professor. 'But maybe,' he said, thinking aloud, 'just maybe the technology could be built into Spy Dog collars. And,' he announced, beaming at Lara, 'it's inventions like this that allow me to make huge amounts of money that can be ploughed back into my Spy Dog training programme. What do you say, GM451?'

Lara couldn't keep her tail still. Her bullet-holed ear stood proudly to attention. *It's a winner, Prof*, she wagged. *And, if you need a volunteer to try it out, semi-retired agent GM451 is at your service.*

Hurtmore Prison

Mr Big went straight to the front of the dinner queue. Nobody dared complain. He was still relatively new to Hurtmore Prison this second time around, but everyone knew who he was. In a prison reserved for the worst of humanity, he was proud to stand out as the most dangerous man there.

He grimaced as food was slopped into the various sections of his plastic plate. His minder took the tray and Mr Big pointed to a table by the window. The prisoners stopped slurping. All eyes turned to the world's most evil criminal. 'Shift,' he grunted and chairs immediately scraped across the floor as eight burly men rose to find another table. 'Except you,' he snarled, nodding at an elderly gentleman with glasses.

'M . . . me?' stammered the prisoner.

'Yes. Y . . . you,' growled Mr Big. 'They call you Nigel "The Knowledge" Barrowclough. You've been inside the longest. And I need some *insider* info.'

Mr Big parked himself opposite 'The Knowledge'. His life of crime had brought him the finer things in life yet here he was, eating slop with common criminals. He consoled himself that it would only be temporary. 'Which celebrity chef cooked this up?' he asked, scooping up a spoonful of something grey and letting it dribble back on to his plate from a great height.

'Cannibal Joe's not a sleb chef,' piped up Nigel. 'But he is famous.'

'Triple murder, so I've heard,' growled the master-criminal. 'And they never found his victims. That's a real talent. He should stick to killing,' he grunted, pushing the bowl away. 'Cooking's not his thing.' The world's most evil man sighed and looked around at the other prisoners. 'It's about time I got acquainted with my neighbours.' He pointed at a large man with a flat face. 'What's he in for?'

'Weeto? Did away with several wives.'

Mr Big looked impressed.

'First wife? Poisoned her cornflakes,' explained The Knowledge. 'Imagine. What a dreadful way to go. And his second? Well, the police weren't quite sure how he did it, but all they would say was that it involved Cheerios and gallons of milk.'

'Nice one,' purred Mr Big. 'A cereal killer. And him?' he said, pointing at a flame-haired man who was pushing food nervously round his plate.

'Ginger Tom,' said The Knowledge knowledgeably. 'Also known as "The Cat Burglar".'

'What's his specialism?' growled Mr Big.

'Er, cats,' said the man hesitantly. 'Steals pedigree moggies and sells them back to their owners. Dead clever that is. Plus he's made a fortune from their collars apparently. Rich owners like their pets to have diamond-encrusted neckwear.'

'Don't we all?' agreed Mr Big.

'And what are you in for, Mr Big?' asked The Knowledge. 'If you don't mind me asking, that is? We know of your reputation. I'm sure you've done hundreds of glorious crimes. Which one are you actually in for?'

Mr Big's mood changed in an instant. 'I'm only in here for one crime,' he snarled. 'Getting caught. And when I get out,' he growled, 'there's going to be one very sorry mutt. And one dead professor.' Everyone said revenge was sweet, but he would have to wait to rid himself of the sour taste of Spy Dog and her evil puppies. His nostrils flared as he looked around at the inmates. The worst criminals from across the land. He had so much in common with his fellow prisoners that he felt sure he was going to enjoy his temporary stay at Hurtmore Prison.

'And what's he in for?' he asked, pointing to his own cellmate, sitting alone at another table.

'I can't get a word of sense out of him. Just jabbers away all day and all night. Keeps mentioning something about the legend of the Nile Ruby.'

'Crazy Dez?' laughed The Knowledge, pointing with one of his good fingers. 'Dr Desmond Farquhar. Your cellmate used to be a famous archaeologist who once met the Queen. But somehow he became a tomb robber. And a serial museum thief.'

Mr Big's eyes widened with interest. 'Tombs and museums, eh? What else do you know?'

'Only that he has broken into the British Museum thirty-four times. Same place. *Thirty-four times!* That's bonkers, that is. And then, the final straw, he was caught in the Egyptian Room, breaking into a coffin. But it wasn't a ruby he was after. He was trying to steal a mummy! Nasty business if you ask me. Imagine trying to steal a dead body. That's just weird, that is.'

Mr Big looked at the old man. He was bony-thin with wild white hair which made him look rather like a spring onion. His eyes darted around as though he was an animal on the run. The old man was chattering to himself. 'He even talks in his sleep,' grumbled the master-criminal. 'Do you think they'll ever let him out?'

'No chance,' smirked The Knowledge. 'This is Hurtmore Ultra. If you do get out, they bring you straight back,' he said, eyeing the only-ever escapee nervously. 'Nobody ever leaves permanently. Unless it's in a coffin.'

Mr Big nodded silently and looked at his frail cellmate, an evil idea forming in his genius mind.

5. A Random Act of Evil

Mr Big returned to his cell. Crazy Dez was scribbling on the wall. Big sidled up to him. 'Tell me again,' he said, this time with genuine interest, 'about this Qua'a bloke. And the ruby.'

'I was a young man back then,' Crazy Dez began, his eyes as wild as his hair. 'In the empty desert, far from the pyramids. We found the tomb,' he smiled, his eyes dancing in their wrinkles. 'But the mummy is cursed. It took my father's life.'

'And the Nile Ruby?' growled Mr Big. 'What is it? And, more importantly, where is it?'

The old man's eyes darted left and then right. He lowered his voice as if someone might be listening. 'Can I trust you?'

A huge smile lit up Mr Big's mouth. 'Man of my word,' he lied.

'The book was right,' whispered the old man. 'Qua'a *was* buried with the world's biggest ruby. I made a terrible mistake.'

'We've all made those, Dr Dez,' agreed Mr Big. 'My mistake was getting caught. And not killing that Spy Dog when I had the chance.'

'I found the tomb. Qua'a was there. He'd been hidden for thousands of years . . .'

'And no jewel,' interrupted Mr Big, trying not to lose his temper. 'Skip the detail, old man. Get to the bit where you tell me where the jewel is.'

'It's written in the stars,' whispered the old man, sweeping his hand round the cell.

'Yeah, well, I can't read the bloomin' stars,' complained Mr Big. 'It's a load of old graffiti.'

'Hieroglyphics,' said the old man.

'Hiero-whatics?'

'The mummy and the ruby are one,' said the old man. 'If you get out of here, you must find the mummy's final resting place. The museum. And it is there that you will find the ruby.'

Silence fell on the cell. Mr Big lay in the top bunk, his brain whirring. His crazy cellmate lay in the bunk below, jabbering away to himself. 'Mad as a box of frogs,' Mr Big murmured under his breath. 'And if he doesn't stop chattering he'll be sending me round the bend too!' The master-criminal looked up at the ceiling. It was covered in strange signs and weird language, scribblings made by his cell-mate. *Men with dogs' heads. Pyramids. Caves. Stars.* Until that moment Mr Big had assumed it was just the graffiti of a madman.

'Stars,' he remembered aloud. 'He said it was written in the stars.'

He looked around at the walls. His cellmate's scribblings were mostly in black felt-tip. In each corner of the cell was a star, coloured in gold. 'Written in the stars,' repeated Mr Big, sitting up with a jolt. He scanned the walls and ceiling again. 'The legend of the Nile Ruby. Useless ramblings of a mad old man. What if they're not?'

'En-*taaar*,' yelled the prison governor.

The door opened and Mr Big was escorted in. His hands were cuffed and he was accompanied by three prison guards. The governor clearly wasn't taking any chances. He was proud to have been promoted to Hurtmore and, while the previous governor was considered a soft touch, he was determined to be the opposite.

'Welcome, Big,' he barked. 'It must be a pleasure for you to make my acquaintance.'

'Yes, sir,' replied Mr Big, faking his best smile. 'I've heard a lot about you.'

'And me you,' snapped the governor. 'And seeing you locked in a cell twenty-three hours a day gives me great pleasure. Not so "*big*" now, are we?' he scoffed.

Mr Big scanned the governor's face, forming an instant dislike. *Tall, grey and serious*, he thought. *Maybe prison governors look like their prisons*. 'I'm a reformed character,' smiled Mr Big, seething on the inside, but remaining calm on

the outside. If he was to get his favour granted then there was no room for error. Killing the governor for real would have to wait. For now Mr Big planned to kill him with kindness.

'And to what do I owe this little visit?' asked the governor.

'Well, sir,' began the world's most cunning villain, 'I'm after a favour . . .'

The governor's belly laugh cut him off.

'Not a favour for me,' corrected Mr Big. 'A favour for my cellmate, Dr Desmond Farquhar, sir. A surprise actually, sir. He's a very old man and I want to do a scrapbook of his life story. For his birthday, sir.' Big paused while this information sunk in. 'He's friends with the Queen, sir,' he reminded the governor.

The governor nodded suspiciously. 'He is indeed, Big. So what exactly is this *favour*?'

'Well, sir, I'd like access to the library. And maybe the computer in the library, sir? Supervised of course. To do some research on my good friend, Dr Farquhar. He used to be a very famous archaeologist. And I thought that I could research his life story and give him the scrapbook for his birthday. A sort of "random act of kindness", sir.'

The governor clasped his fingers together and pondered. Big was famous for doing random acts of evil. 'Why the sudden desire to do good?' he asked.

'I figure that I'm stuck here for the rest of my days,' said Mr Big. 'No chance of escape,' he lied. 'It'd be stupid to even try,' he lied again. 'So I've turned over a new leaf, sir,' he beamed, delivering a triple-fib. 'And I'd be doing you a good turn too,' he reminded the governor. 'Because you'll get yourself an OBE. Or a knighthood, sir. For getting me to change my ways.'

'Rehabilitated,' said the governor, rolling the 'R'. There was some merit in what Big was saying. Farquhar did indeed know the Queen. 'Changing your ways? A knighthood, you say?'

Mr Big was marched out of the governor's office. Keeping Big locked up was the governor's basic requirement. Getting him to change his ways would be a major bonus that would alert the Home Secretary and Prime Minister. *Thirty minutes' Internet a day couldn't do any harm.*

Big couldn't hide a grin as he was accompanied back to his cell. His charm offensive had worked.

★

Mr Big booked himself into the prison library. His Internet access was closely monitored. He Googled 'Egyptians' and cursed. *52 million references*. Even his life sentence wasn't long enough to investigate all those. He tapped 'Desmond Farquhar' into the search engine. Then narrowed it down to 'Dr Desmond Farquhar, Egyptologist'. He clicked on the first few references and started jotting down some notes.

Mr Big checked his watch. He was allowed thirty minutes' Internet a day. 'Doesn't time fly when you're having fun?' he snarled to himself. He had two minutes left as he entered his final Internet search: 'The legend of the Nile Ruby'.

6. Dead Easy!

'It can't be that time already,' whined Ollie, as Mum helped him into his coat.

'The professor's a very busy man,' explained Mum. 'And you've had a whole day with him. I'm sure he's got better things to do than chatter to a bunch of kids and dogs.'

The professor pondered Mrs Cook's comment. There were nearly six hundred things on his 'to do' list, but he couldn't think of a single one that he'd rather do than spend time with his beloved GM451. And, if that meant the children came as part of the package, that was fine. He opened his mouth to explain this to Mrs Cook, but was cut off before he had the chance to start.

'So say thank you to Professor Cortex and we'll be on our way.'

'Thank you,' mumbled Ollie, sad to be leaving.

Ben shook the old man's hand and Sophie hugged him tightly.

'Careful, young lady,' gasped the scientist. 'Oxygen and all that. Keeps me alive.'

Spud and Star saluted. 'Our hero,' woofed Star.

Lara sat and waited until everyone else had turned to leave. *Why do I find goodbyes so difficult?* She knew the professor's world was one of constant peril. *He's got the best brain on the planet*, she thought, *so there are bound to be enemy agents eyeing him up*.

Lara sat and offered her paw. The professor bent down and shook it politely. 'Thank you for popping by to see me,' he said. 'You've made an old man very . . . *ahem* . . .' He dabbed a tissue at his eyes . . . 'happy. It's so pleasing to see how you've settled into family life.'

Family life's brill, nodded Lara. *I like being a pet. And I really appreciate you sharing your gadgets with us*.

'You are my greatest achievement, GM451,' croaked the professor, his voice breaking with emotion. 'And it's thanks to you that Mr Big is locked up somewhere safe and we can all sleep well at night.'

Mr Big hadn't slept well. He sat in the canteen, watching the prisoners queuing for their slop. He knew that Cannibal Joe had been a chef on the outside, but he questioned the decision to put him in charge of the cooking. The name alone was unnerving, but just one look at Joe told you that hygiene wasn't his top priority. Mr Big played with his porridge as he watched Joe scratching his sweat patches. Cannibal Joe stopped serving for a second as he squeezed a spot, the yellow pus squirting into the porridge. Joe cheerfully mixed it in.

Mr Big felt some sick rise in the back of his throat. He pushed his bowl away and turned to a greasy plate of sausage and scrambled egg. *Cannibal Joe?* He imagined the sausages might be fingers. He wasn't sure he could face them so he peered out of the window and watched as a hearse pulled into the grounds of the prison. Four prison guards emerged and heaved a cheap-looking coffin into the back of the vehicle.

One of the prison kitchen team approached Mr Big. 'You've not finished your special porridge,' he said, a note of disappointment in his voice.

'No appetite,' growled Mr Big. 'This place is beginning to get to me. I need out.'

The prisoner followed Big's gaze and they watched as the coffin was loaded into the hearse. The prison gates opened and the car drove solemnly away.

'Another one gone,' laughed the prisoner. 'That's the only way you're ever going to get out of here, Big. In your coffin.'

Mr Big's heart was pounding. All of a sudden he felt hungry. He sawed off a chunk of gristly sausage and looked up at his fellow prisoner. 'What an excellent idea.'

Mr Big possessed the two most important characteristics for a master-criminal: 'evil' and 'genius'. And, although he was behind bars, he still had power. He knew one of the inmates who worked in the pharmacy and managed to get hold of the pills by the next day.

'For your nerves, old man,' he said, offering Dr Desmond two pills. He held a cup of water in the other hand. 'Get yourself a good night's sleep.'

The old man looked grateful. Allowing the Nile Ruby to slip through his hands was a mistake that had haunted him for a lifetime. He shoved the pills into his mouth and swigged the water. 'Sweet Egyptian dreams,' growled Mr Big.

Dr Desmond lay down silently in the bottom bunk. His breathing stopped almost immediately.

Mr Big hardly slept a wink. His brain whirred with ideas and he knew that morning would be a big test. At first light he rose from his bed and took pictures of the cell wall on a stolen mobile phone. He emailed the pictures to himself and flushed the phone down the toilet. Then, just before 8 a.m., the hatch slid open and the guard's face leered in.

Mr Big fixed the guard with his saddest eyes. 'The old man has died.'

It was early afternoon when Big's chance came. The empty coffin had arrived and Dr Desmond's stiff body had been loaded in. Mr Big pretended to be distraught. 'My cellmate,' he whimpered. 'We'd become very close. The old man was like a father to me. May I have a minute alone?'

The guard shifted uneasily. His orders were clear. 'Never take your eyes off Big,' the governor had warned. 'And don't trust a thing he says.' Mr Big had bribed one of the prisoners to hit the fire alarm at 2 p.m. precisely. He managed to stay sad on the outside, but his heart was thumping as he eyed the clock ticking towards the allotted second. *Yes!* His heart leapt with joy. *Right on time!*

'That's the fire alarm,' yelled one of the guards. Both guards backed out of Mr Big's cell and ran down the corridor.

Mr Big was calm. He lifted the coffin lid and pulled the old man out by his arms. He hauled him into the top bunk and pulled the blankets over. Then he climbed inside the coffin and made himself comfortable before closing the lid. Mr Big looked at his luminous watch and grinned in the dark. 'I'll be out in an hour,' he whispered.

The alarm was switched off and the guards returned. Mr Big was a tough cookie so neither wanted to wake him. The coffin was carried down several flights of stairs and Mr Big spent an hour in the prison chapel while the chaplain muttered a few prayers. The coffin was then hauled into the back of a hearse and driven away from Hurtmore Prison.

Mr Big lay in the darkness, grinning the grin

of an evil genius. 'I am now the only person
ever to have escaped from ultra-security prison.
Twice!'

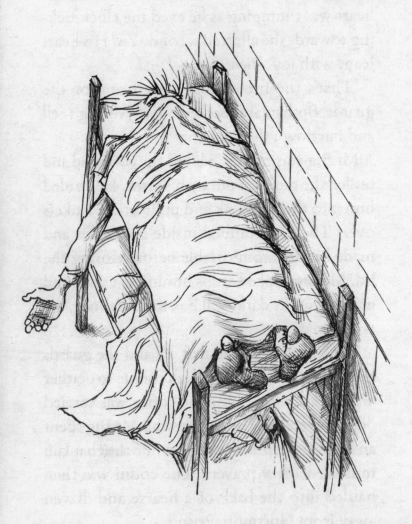

7. The Living Dead

It was lunchtime and the gravedigger couldn't believe his luck. It was such a rare treat to be sitting by the fire in his favourite pub on a work day! He watched the rain pelting down. He was on his fourth pint of his unexpected day off. He had an envelope of crisp twenties in his back pocket, with a note. 'Ring in sick,' Mr Big had written. 'No graves to be filled in today.' He looked at the foul weather outside and sauntered back to the bar. 'One more, please, my good man,' he slurred, 'and some pork scratchings.'

Fifty metres away the vicar stood under an umbrella, sheltering his prayer book from the wet. The coffin had been lowered into the ground and he muttered a few words. 'Ashes to ashes . . . whatever to whatever,' he began. He looked up at the grey sky and then down at the hole in the ground. He considered it a double whammy. *Bad weather plus the dead man is a prisoner. It's no wonder there isn't a single relative at the funeral.* He pulled up his cassock and hurried back to the warmth of the vicarage.

It was 9 p.m. before the landlord decided to stop serving. 'Come on, Albert,' he soothed, wrapping the gravedigger's coat round his shoulders. 'You've had one too many. Best you get off home.'

Albert didn't live far away, but the zigzagging tripled the distance. He'd forgotten exactly how many pints of beer he'd drunk, but most of the crisp twenties had gone. He took his usual short cut past the church, staggering through the graveyard.

The most evil man in the world counted patience as one of his best qualities. Just behind 'evil', 'menace' and 'brutality'. He checked the luminous dial of his watch: *9 p.m.* The rain had turned to drizzle and he knew that it would be dark outside. He also knew that the guards would soon work out what was going on. *They'll have found the dead Dr Desmond Farquhar in my bed. And, even though they're incredibly stupid, they'll be putting two and two together.*

The coffin lid creaked open and Mr Big looked up at the night sky. Light rain fell on to his face and he grinned an evil grin. It was great to be on the outside. He scrambled out of the grave, muddy and wet.

The gravedigger stood and watched as the fingernails clawed at the earth and the soil-covered man rose from the dead.

'Evening,' mumbled Mr Big.

The gravedigger dropped his kebab.

'Swapsies,' growled the dead man. 'I'll be needing your clothes and then in you go,' he said, pointing down to the empty coffin.

The gravedigger was regretting the last half-dozen drinks. He knew there was no way you should argue with someone rising from the dead. He clambered down into the hole and sat in the coffin in his pants.

'Close it.' The lid slammed shut and the grave-digger was glad to be somewhere safe and warm.

The dead man hobbled away into the night.

'Sit upright,' woofed Lara to Spud. 'Your tummy's sagging.'

The puppy breathed in, making an effort to hold his belly in. He was excited because this was a special day and he was sure there would be special food.

Lara thought Mum and Dad looked nervous. Ollie had been pointing at all the portraits and asking who they were. 'Thatcher,' explained Dad, recognizing the only picture of a woman. 'And Churchill,' he noted, spotting the famous 'V for Victory' sign.

'I thought Churchill was a dog,' exclaimed Ollie, looking puzzled.

'*Winston* Churchill was a very famous British prime minister,' said Mum. 'In fact, all those pictures are of prime ministers.'

Ollie's fizzy drink had kicked in. *Everything's exciting when you're six*, smiled Lara as the little boy sprinted to the window.

'And why are the police stopping all those people from coming down this street?' he asked.

'We've got special permission,' explained Sophie. 'This is Downing Street, where the Prime Minister lives. And this is Number Ten. His *actual* house.'

Lara looked round at her family. *I'm so proud*, she thought. *The pups are so happy to have the kids. And the kids so happy to have the pups. And don't the children look splendid in what Mum calls their 'Sunday best'?* Lara wondered why they'd been summoned to Number Ten. *We've met him before*, she recalled. *It might be good news*, she hoped, thinking of a possible community award for the pups. *We have slashed crime in our neighbourhood.*

Lara was snapped out of her thoughts as the PM's door opened and the Cook family were ushered into his office. Professor Cortex was already there, looking a little nervous. *Not good*, thought Lara, her instincts taking over.

There was no time to chat because the PM swept in. Lara couldn't help but notice that he also looked rather nervous. 'Please take a seat,' he said. Mum and Dad chose luxury red leather armchairs. Sophie and Ben sat on the edge of the big sofa. Ollie leapt on to the other sofa and bounced up and down until he caught his mother's glare.

Lara and the professor preferred to stand.

'Mr and Mrs Cook,' began the Prime Minister, 'I'm afraid I have some, erm, news.'

'What kind of "news"?' demanded Mrs Cook.

'Not particularly good news, I'm afraid,' winced the PM. 'It's Mr Big, you see,' he stammered, glancing at Mrs Cook.

'What do I see?' she enquired as the PM suddenly felt hot under the collar.

'He's . . . you know . . .' He glanced at Professor Cortex, his eyes pleading for help.

'Escaped,' blurted the professor. 'Gone and done it again! Not my fault this time,' added the scientist, wincing at a bad memory. 'The

police found a dead man in his bed and a naked gravedigger in a coffin, and . . .'

'We think we know where he is,' interrupted the Prime Minister, scrabbling for some good news.

'Well, capture him then!' blurted Mrs Cook. 'He's evil. And he's after revenge.' All eyes fell on the family pet. 'On Lara.'

'Quite,' added the PM. 'If only it was that easy.'

Lara looked round at her adopted family. *I chose well*, she considered. *They are fiercely loyal to me*. She looked at the youngest, Ollie. He was jumping on the sofa, shooting imaginary bullets at the imaginary Mr Big. Sophie was biting her bottom lip. Ben patted Lara's head reassuringly. *I'm officially the family pet*, she thought, *but Ben is my best buddy*.

Lara hadn't always been a family pet. She thought back to her Spy Dog days. *Adventure, excitement, missions . . . saving the world. But then it all went horribly wrong*. Her mind sped back to her first encounter with the evil Mr Big. *In a forest. He had a gun and all I had was my Spy Dog training. I took some bullets*, she thought, her paw touching the hole in her sticky-up ear. *But he came off worse. Teeth marks in his backside*, she grinned. *And a life sentence.*

'Letting him escape once is bad enough,' said Mrs Cook, her finger waving at the PM just like it did at the children. 'But twice is just . . . well . . .'

'Criminal?' offered Ollie, bouncing up and down.

'Exactly,' she snarled. 'So where is he? You said you know where he is. So where *exactly* is he?'

The PM smoothed his hair and sat down. 'Let's all relax,' he said, looking specifically at Mrs Cook. 'We have a plan to recapture Big.' Everyone immediately seemed at ease. 'But,' he said, looking the retired Spy Dog in the eye, 'we need your help.'

8. Mission Impossible?

A man came into the room with a pot of coffee and some juice. Another man wheeled in a trolley and Spud eyed the plates of food, his eyes on stalks. *Cheese and pickled onions, on sticks*, he wagged. *Only my fave thing in the whole entire universe!* Drinks were poured while a lady in a sharp suit set up a projector and laptop. Lara took a sip of her juice and the PM pressed a button.

'GM451,' began the PM. Lara shook her head. *Retired Spy Dog*, she thought. *Plain old Lara now, thank you very much*. She took a pencil in her mouth and wrote 'LARA' on a pad in front of her before pawing it across to the Prime Minister.

'Lara,' he smiled, 'I would like to personally apologize. We are searching for a new governor of Hurtmore Prison. And we are, of course, *ahem*, searching for the world's most terrible criminal mastermind. However, we don't want to scare the public, so we have kept Big's escape out of the news. If it were to leak out, then there would be panic on the streets. So hush-hush,' he said, tapping his nose. 'Mum's the word,' he smiled, casting a glance at Mrs Cook. 'Top-secret stuff.'

'You said you knew where he was,' said Ben.

The PM raised a nervous eyebrow. He pressed a button and a fuzzy picture was beamed on to the screen.

'Here's our man,' said Professor Cortex, taking up the story. 'Not the best quality pic, but this shows Big at the British Museum. The dark glasses and beard are an attempt at a disguise, but it's him all right.'

It was the PM's turn. 'The police were called, but Big had disappeared before they arrived. But he's been there twice in the last two days. To the same part of the museum actually. The Egyptian Room.'

Lara put her paw to her head and scratched. *Why would he risk being caught out in the open?* she thought. *He must know there are CCTV cameras at the museum.*

Another picture was beamed on to the screen. It was a black and white image of a handsome young man. 'This one is an oldie,' said the professor. 'It shows Big's cellmate, Dr Desmond Farquhar, in the desert. He spent a lifetime searching for the so-called Nile Ruby. While the world marvelled at the pyramids, he had a theory that the Egyptians had actually buried their most precious artefacts far away from them.' He studied the puzzled expressions around him. 'Basically, he thought the pyramids were a decoy.' The professor paused, his eyebrows creased into a frown. 'Kind of makes sense, if you think about it. Why would you erect a huge pyramid which basically advertises where your jewels are?'

The Prime Minister clicked again. 'And this was Dr Farquhar just before he died.' There was a sharp intake of breath as the spring onion old man in prison uniform was beamed on to the screen.

'I can't believe it's the same man,' gasped Sophie. 'He looks wild. And his eyes are kind of crazy-looking.'

'Crazy indeed,' agreed Professor Cortex. 'At least that's what most people thought. We think he was probably driven mad because he'd found out where the Nile Ruby was, but was unable to get at it.'

'What was he in prison for?' asked Ben. 'He doesn't look dangerous.'

The PM looked down at his notes. 'He broke into the British Museum thirty-four times. On the final occasion there was a terrible accident and one of the guards was killed. So our man went down for murder. And whatever he was trying to steal has remained a secret.'

'Until now,' said Professor Cortex. 'He'd made notes on his cell wall. Mostly in hiero-glyphics, which is the ancient language of the Egyptians. As Edward — I mean, the Prime Minister, said, most people thought he was mad, what with his tales of mummies, long-lost legends, rubies and whatever else. But,' he said, glancing at the PM, 'what if he wasn't?'

Lara's eyes widened with interest. Even Spud took his eyes off the cheese and pickle for a second.

'You mean, what if the legend of the Nile Ruby is true?' gasped Ben.

'Remember, this man spent time with Mr Big. And there's something that we haven't told you. The old man was poisoned. And, since his escape, Big has been spotted at the *same* museum. *Twice*. The bits of the jigsaw seem to be fitting together.'

The professor pointed at the big screen where there were images of the old man's cell wall. 'I've examined his writing,' he said, looking over the top of his spectacles. 'Very interesting indeed. In ancient times, the richest Egyptians were buried with their possessions.'

'So they could use them in the afterlife,' continued Ben. 'We did it in history.'

'Then you'll also know about the mummification process,' said the professor.

Ben's eyes lit up. 'I know that they used to remove the internal organs. Heart and lungs and stuff.'

'And that they pulled their brains out through their noses,' added Ollie, yanking an imaginary brain from his left nostril.

'Well,' said Professor Cortex, 'from the writing on his cell wall, it seems that the Nile Ruby was in fact buried with Qua'a.' He clicked a button on the laptop and a magnified picture lit up the screen. 'This was drawn on the cell wall. See the dog's head?'

Human and dog heads nodded.

'That represents Qua'a. And see what's *inside* the head?'

The professor magnified the image further still.

'Looks like a diamond?' suggested Sophie, squinting at the blurry image.

'A ruby actually,' nodded the professor. 'This is what drove Dr Farquhar mad. He searched the cave for the ruby, but couldn't find it. The one place he didn't look was *inside* the mummy. According to Dr Desmond's theory, the brain had been removed and replaced with the ruby! Don't you see?' jabbered the professor, his glasses sliding down his nose in excitement. 'It was the only place he *didn't* look.'

'Yuk,' said Sophie. 'So the most expensive jewel in the world is inside the head of the mummy.'

'Which explains why Dr Farquhar tried to break in thirty-four times,' gasped Ben.

'And why Mr Big is now trying to break in,' added Sophie.

'So why are we here?' asked Ben.

'I need a favour,' began the PM. 'From GM451 and the Spy Pups actually.'

Lara lifted an eyebrow at the Prime Minister.

'I . . . I mean *Lara* and her pups,' he corrected. 'I would like Britain's finest canine spies to recapture Mr Big.'

Spud's head jerked away from the food trolley and he nearly fell off his seat with excitement. *A mission!*

Star wagged her tail so hard it banged on the PM's desk.

Lara looked less sure. *Spy Dog . . . retired*, she

thought. *I don't do danger any more, remember?*

The professor mopped his brow. 'Mr Big's escape has been kept secret,' he said. 'To stop the public from panicking. We think he's after the ruby but, quite frankly, there's no telling what he might do next. And, as I'm sure you realize, he has a rather large grudge against GM451 and the Cook family.'

We did capture him, wagged Lara with a satisfied doggie grin on her face.

'You mean he might come after *us*?' said Sophie, her eyes full of fear.

'Not if we can recapture him,' noted the PM. 'We can't flood the museum with police or Big will know we're on to him. He'd disappear and that would be . . . fatal,' he said, regretting the choice of word. 'He doesn't know we're on to him and that's how it needs to remain,' he added gravely. 'This has to be top secret. Three Spy Dogs against one arch-criminal. Of course, if anything went wrong, my government would have to deny all knowledge.'

'Like *Mission Impossible*?' yapped Spud.

'Should we choose to accept it,' warned Lara.

'Please, Ma,' yapped Star. 'We'd be helping to protect our beloved family. Let's do what the PM wants. Let's get that horrible man back behind bars, where he belongs.'

Lara looked at her puppies and then at the children. She weighed up the danger of Mr Big tracking them down versus the danger of trying to capture him at the museum. Her heart pounded with excitement. She nodded at the PM. *This Spy Dog is available for one last mission.*

9. Terror Thomas

The children were irritated that they weren't going to be part of the mission, but it was just too dangerous with Mr Big on the rampage. They spent the day with their parents, cooped up in a London hotel, while Professor Cortex and the puppies did some surveillance. 'Dogs aren't allowed in the museum,' he told Lara. 'But these little guys can sneak into my backpack and I'll go in as a tourist. We'll investigate the Egyptian Room and check out the security situation.'

Professor Cortex was the world's best scientist, but his skills didn't stretch to spying. He was sweating as he walked up the steps to the British Museum, partly because it was a hot day, partly because his backpack was heavy, but mostly because he was a rubbish liar. He knew if anyone asked him what was in his backpack he'd panic and admit to two stowaway puppies. The surveillance mission would have to be abandoned if that happened, and they needed to know the layout of the museum to have the best chance of taking Big on. 'Quit fidgeting, you two,' he said out of the corner of his mouth. 'We're entering the museum.'

Spud and Star lay still. Each had eyeholes cut into the backpack so they could see out, but nobody could see in. *Perfect for spying*.

Lara was on the roof opposite, her binoculars trained on the museum. 'All clear,' she woofed into the headset. The professor heard Star give two muffled yaps from the backpack and knew the coast was clear. He breezed through reception a little too confidently, walking fast and whistling. He nodded nervously at the security guard, who nodded back. *Don't look guilty. Don't look guilty.* The professor and his puppy spies climbed the marble staircase and entered the inner sanctum of the Egyptian Room. He held his camera to his face and clicked. 'We're in,' he whispered into the hidden microphone. The pups peered out of the backpack, looking for clues. Star was scanning the visitors, looking for Mr Big. Spud was looking for discarded sandwiches.

Lara watched them through her powerful binoculars. *The professor's sweat is visible from a hundred metres!* 'Security,' she woofed. 'Coming down the stairs towards you.' One muffled puppy whine signalled trouble and the professor stopped and looked closely at the nearest exhibit, peering in, pretending to read all about it. The security guard wandered past and Professor Cortex breathed a sigh of relief. He pointed his camera at the CCTV cameras and clicked. 'At least three cameras,' he reported to Lara, listening in from across the road.

'You've been spotted,' woofed Lara into the microphone. 'A guard is coming straight for you.' She checked the list of faces that the professor had downloaded from the Internet and matched the guard against the pictures. 'Looks like the head of security,' she whined. 'Major Anthony Thomas. Not good.'

Star signalled trouble with a short, muffled whimper and the professor stopped nervously in his tracks. He jumped as a hand fell on to his shoulder. 'Good afternoon, sir,' said a voice. 'Enjoying the exhibition?'

The professor turned to see a short man with a peaked cap. One eye seemed to be looking directly at the professor and the other had wandered off somewhere behind him. *False eye?* wondered the professor.

The head of security noticed the man was sweating, yet the museum was air-conditioned.

'Very warm,' grinned the scientist. He'd spent his life in a laboratory and was wishing he'd spent just a little more time learning about being a spy.

'Interested in history, sir?' questioned the security guard.

'Oh yes,' stammered the professor. 'Especially Egypt. Absolutely fascinating stuff. Went there on holiday once,' he said, trying to sound enthusiastic. 'Did a Nile cruise. They do the most magnificent kebabs, you know.'

Lara put her paw to her head. *We're casing the joint, searching for clues, and the prof decides to make polite conversation with the head of security!*

'If you're dead keen, sir, you'll know that the museum has a special Egyptian Room. It's where we keep all the good stuff,' added the head of security.

'Ooh goody,' nodded the professor a little too enthusiastically. 'I'll most definitely be going there. To the spying . . . I mean *special* room. I love history so much I wish I could live here,' he said, a silly grin fixed to his face.

Lara's heart was pounding. *He's babbling.* She knew she could give word and abort the mission at any time.

'I more or less do live here,' boasted the

guard. 'Perk of the job. This card gets me access to all areas. Even the parts of the museum that tourists can't reach.' He held up his securiy card and the professor looked a little too closely.

'Nice picture,' he beamed, 'Mr Thomas.'

'You seem very interested in security,' noted the guard. 'I noticed you were taking pictures,' he said, one eye boring into the professor, the other looking into the middle distance.

The professor wasn't sure which was his good eye. He glanced behind himself warily, just to see what the other eye was looking at. 'Yes, yes,' he beamed, still a little too enthusiastically. 'Pictures of mummies and all that.'

'Except, sir,' noted the guard, 'I saw you taking pictures of the security control panel and the CCTV cameras. And, I was wondering, who would come to the British Museum and take pictures of the cameras? If you don't mind me saying, that seems a little odd, sir.'

'Odd . . .' began the professor, his brain whirring but his mouth unsure what was going to come out. 'I also like CCTV cameras, you see. Two hobbies. That's it. Egypt and security cameras. I've got hundreds of pictures of them. Quite beautiful . . .'

Spud couldn't help snorting with laughter. Star slammed her paw across his mouth and the professor felt the bag wriggle. He was sure the guard's good eye had spotted it so tried to end the conversation.

Lara had made her mind up. 'Abort. Abort,' she woofed into the microphone. The retired Spy Dog started packing her surveillance equipment away, ready for a quick getaway.

'Anyway,' sweated the professor, 'must go. I've got to take some pics of the CCTV cameras outside Buck Palace. Beauties,' he said, smiling and backing away. 'Made in Germany, you know.'

The guard's hand came down on the backpack. 'If you don't mind, sir, I'll just take a peek inside. Make sure you're not making off with anything.'

The professor panicked. He wriggled out of his backpack and started to run. The guard wasn't sure what to do. He clicked the bag open and two puppies leapt out. The man jumped, the bag fell to the floor and Spud and Star were away. Star overtook the professor on the stairs, saluting him as she slid down the bannister. Spud yelped loudly. *Create a diversion*. He snapped at the guard's ankles until he dropped his walkie-talkie. *Make as much noise as possible*, he remembered his mum telling him. The guard reached for his radio, but it was smashed.

Tourists started running and panic spread through the museum. By the time 'Terror' Thomas regained control, the professor was doubled up, hands on his knees, sucking in lungfuls of air. He'd made it to the rendezvous point in Hyde Park. Star and Lara were with him. Spud had exited out of the museum cafe, snaffling a cream cake on the way. He trotted up to the gang, cream splattered round his nose.

'How did I do?' gasped the professor.

Star wagged hard and Spud licked the last of the cream off his whiskers. Lara grabbed a pencil and notepad. 'We need access to all areas,' scribbled the dog. 'We need Thomas's security card.'

10. The All-seeing Eye

The professor had called an emergency mission meeting for himself and the dogs. Ben was annoyed that the children were banned. He stormed into the professor's hotel suite with his angry face on.

'There's no point, Benjamin,' warned the professor, holding his hand in the air for calm.

Lara nodded. *He's absolutely right*, she thought. *This is far too dangerous for you guys. Mr Big is the most evil villain on the planet and he has a personal vendetta against all of us. For once, you kids will have to sit this one out.*

'It's more than my life's worth,' said the professor. 'This is a top-secret mission, requested by the Prime Minister. Please, Benjamin, leave it to the experts.'

Ben managed to look mildly irritated as he

turned and slammed the door. He always knew they'd throw him out. 'Which is why I phoned you, Soph. Just before I stormed into the meeting. And hid my mobile behind a cushion,' he grinned to his brother and sister. 'So we can listen in!'

Sophie pressed the loudspeaker button on her mobile and the children crowded round. The professor was in full flow. 'Big has been seen in the museum for the last two days,' he reminded the Spy Dogs. 'And my best guess is that something will happen sooner rather than later. Most probably tonight when the museum is closed and there are no pesky tourists to get in his way,' he suggested. The scientist had loaded the museum layout on to his tablet computer. 'So GM451 and I have hatched a plan to get inside the museum after hours. Once inside, we will wait for Big to strike and capture him red-handed.'

Lara wagged her tail, but she was feeling less than confident. *I doubt it's going to be quite as easy as it sounds*, she thought.

'The museum is patrolled at night,' said the professor. 'By two security guards. The security room is here,' he said, tapping a finger at a box in the middle of the diagram. 'CCTV control room. That means if we get access to this we can see the whole building. So this is where we need to be.'

'That'll be mission control,' woofed Lara to the puppies. 'Where we watch and wait.'

Star took a pencil in her mouth and tapped on a laptop. 'How do we get into the museum when all the doors will be locked?' read the words.

Ben rubbed his hands in glee as he heard the professor's voice. 'We steal Thomas's security card. He was right – it gives access to all areas. And that's exactly what we need.'

'Sounds doable,' yapped Star. 'That disables the alarm and gets us into the CCTV control room, right, Mum?'

Lara nodded.

'Just one minor problem,' said the professor, raising an eyebrow. 'You see from the pictures I got that entry to the CCTV control room is also by retina recognition.'

In the room next door, Ollie looked confused. 'What's a retina?' he shrugged.

'Part of your eye,' hushed Ben.

'So they're doomed,' whispered Sophie to

her brothers. 'They'll never get in because they need Thomas's card and Thomas himself.'

'Shush,' whispered Ben, putting his finger to his lips and straining to listen to the conversation next door.

'GM451 has done some splendid investigative work. She checked him out in the flesh and medical records confirm it. Anthony Thomas, aka "Terror Thomas" on account of his booming voice, is ex-military. Retired due to ill health nine years ago. Lost an eye in Iraq. I suspect his glass eye will be in a jar by his bed. Get our hands on that and it's game on.'

It was 9 p.m. when the professor, Lara and the puppies left the hotel. The professor had explained once again that it was far too dangerous for children. 'I know you'll be disappointed,' he explained to the crestfallen trio. 'But you've had more adventures than most children have had hot dinners.' Spud's ears pricked up at the sound of food. 'Our plan is top secret. All I can tell you is that it involves some breaking and entering and there's a high probability that we'll encounter Mr Big himself.' The professor shuddered.

I'll keep you in the loop, thought Lara, grabbing the professor's hand and making it into the shape of a hand phone. *Any excitement, we'll give you a bell*.

Ben had ordered Ollie to look upset. He was sobbing as Lara tucked him into bed. The family pet blew him a kiss as she closed the bedroom door. She was sad that the children were upset, but thrilled at the prospect of capturing Mr Big.

Five seconds later Ollie was grinning, Ben congratulating him on his Oscar-winning performance. He looked at his watch. 'We'll meet them at the museum at midnight,' he smiled.

★

Lara had persuaded the professor to sit out phase one. She figured that he'd be a liability in Terror Thomas's house, so he sat in his van and watched as the pups approached. It was 11 p.m., an hour since Terror Thomas's bedroom light had gone off. They knew he lived alone. Star had squeezed in through the cat flap and opened the door. The three dogs stood in the hallway, nostrils twitching for clues and their eyes making sense of the dark. 'There's no telling where his security card will be,' reminded Lara. 'Let's search the ground floor first.'

Star took the lounge, silently sniffing round the sofa and armchairs. Lara tiptoed into the dining room before exploring the downstairs toilet. Predictably, Spud took the kitchen. He sniffed the fruit bowl and the kitchen table. He snaffled a small piece of bacon that had fallen behind the cooker. *Maybe he keeps his security card in the fridge*, thought the sharp-minded pup. He leapt at the fridge door and it creaked open. *You never know*, he thought. A dim light lit up the kitchen. Spud spied some cheese. *And some ham! And looky here . . . pickled onions! My fave.*

He carefully removed the jar from the fridge and pushed the door shut. He unscrewed the lid and stuck his paw into the cool vinegar. He was drooling. Pickled onions had overtaken donuts as his absolute favourite food. He popped a pickle into his mouth and crunched. His eyes went gaga as the tangy onion exploded in his mouth. *But no sign of a security card*, he thought to himself as he met his mum and his sister outside in the hallway. Lara looked disapprovingly at her son's jar of pickles. 'Midnight snack,' he announced. 'Spying burns up calories!'

The dogs crept upstairs. Logic said the card and glass eye would be in Thomas's bedroom so all three dogs nosed their way in. The head of security was snoring gently. Lara tapped her paws along his jacket pocket. 'Bingo!' she whined, jabbing a paw at the garment. Star stuck her long nose in and pulled out the card.

Spud was over by the bed. Big red digits said it was 11.56. *Nearly midnight. Time for another snack*, he grinned, tossing a pickle into his mouth. *There it is*, he thought, spotting the glass beside the bed. It was dark but his keen doggie eyesight picked out the round outline of the glass eye, keeping moist in a glass of water. The puppy jabbed his vinegary paw into

the jar and slithered it around after the eye.
Gotcha! thought the puppy. *And, just so he doesn't
wake up and notice, I'll replace it with a pickled
onion*. He plopped an eye-sized pickle into the
glass and retreated to the landing.

Star held up the card, Spud the glass eye.

'Phase one accomplished,' whined Lara as
the dogs made their escape.

11. Museum Mayhem

It was a few minutes past midnight, but London was still buzzing although the museum was in darkness. 'There should be nobody in there,' said the professor, 'except two security guards. This security card and eye will give us access to the CCTV control room. And from there we can monitor the whole building. If Big is going to break in, we'll be able to track his every move and corner him as soon as he's got hold of the mummy. He'll be caught red-handed! And, even better, we'll have him on film.'

The professor approached the back door of the museum. He looked around nervously as he inserted the security card into the slot. A green light lit up and the lock was deactivated. Lara nosed the door open and the professor was just about to follow her inside when three children emerged from the shadows. 'Don't forget us,' piped up Ollie, scampering towards the open door. The professor nearly dropped the card in surprise. 'Oliver,' he began. 'And Benjamin and Sophie. What on earth are you doing here?'

'What do you think?' beamed Ollie. 'Ben says you're having an adventure. And we always share adventures with you.'

'Well, you jolly well can't share this one,' hissed the scientist. 'It's top secret. And danger-ous. And your mother would kill me if she found out.' The professor was sweating. He couldn't let the children into the museum. But it was equally dangerous to lock them out and let them wander the streets of London with Mr Big on the prowl.

'Mum won't find out,' said Ben. 'We know the plan. We're better spies than you think! All we want is to stay hidden in the CCTV room while you and the dogs catch the evil Mr Big.'

'He's our family's worst enemy,' reminded Sophie. 'He even shot our dog. So it's only right that we should watch him being recaptured.'

Lara was listening intently, her sticky-up ear standing tall. She watched shadowy figures walk past the museum. *The streets of London are surprisingly busy at night*, she thought. *No place for children. Maybe the high-security CCTV room is the best place for the kids to be. And there's no time to waste,* she thought. *Mr Big might already be here!* Lara decided to take a calculated risk. She tugged Ben by the coat and ushered him through the door.

'See,' smiled the boy, 'Lara thinks it's all right.'

The professor chuntered under his breath as Sophie and Ollie came in too. 'I hope you know what you're doing, GM451,' he huffed as the door shut and the small gang was locked in the museum. The professor fumbled for his tablet computer. He switched it on and the low glow lit up the hallway. He clicked to the diagram of the museum. 'We're here,' he said, tapping the blue dot. 'And the security room is here. So it's this way,' he said, his finger pointing up some stairs. 'First floor, next to Neolithic man.'

The professor, children and dogs tiptoed up the stairs, the tablet providing the only light. At the top of the stairs the blue dot showed they needed to turn left. Ben fumbled in his backpack for a torch. He clicked it on. He shone the light on an exhibit and Sophie stifled a squeal.

Yikes, thought Lara. *That caveman exhibit is very realistic!*

'Looks a bit like Dad,' suggested Ollie. 'And that one looks like Grandma Edith,' he said, pointing at a Neolithic woman with sunken eyes and a beard.

The posse made its way to the security room. 'Let's see if we can get in,' said the professor, handing the computer to Ollie. He rummaged in his pocket and held up the security card in one hand and the glass eye in the other. 'Wish me luck!' He swiped the card against the lock. The light went green. 'Retina scan required,' purred an electronic voice. A small screen lit up, at the professor's eye level. 'Here goes,' he said, holding Terror Thomas's eye up to the screen.

'Scanning,' announced the electronic voice. 'Thomas approved.' The door clicked open and Lara nosed her way into the security room.

Ben punched the air in delight. 'Great plan, Lara,' he said. 'We're in!'

'There are no windows so we can switch the light on,' said the professor. 'Only Terror Thomas ever comes in here so we're safe.' Ben and the professor switched on every CCTV monitor and black and white images lit up the screens.

'There's one of the guards,' said Sophie,

pointing to a screen. The professor tapped a button and the camera zoomed in to get a closer look at a man asleep on a sofa.

'Sleeping on the job,' mumbled the professor disapprovingly. He started to make a note in his book. 'You just can't get the staff nowadays.'

'He's not sleeping,' said Ben. 'He's unconscious. Look at his hands. He's handcuffed to the sofa!'

Oh deary me, thought Lara as she spotted the other guard. She tapped a screen to her right and everyone looked. It was quite a dark image, but they could make out another unconscious man lying on the floor.

'He's asleep as well,' gasped Sophie. 'And he's stripped down to his vest and boxers!'

'I don't think he's asleep,' shrugged the professor. 'Mr Big's coshed him and stolen his uniform. Which suggests our arch-enemy is in the building.' He mopped his brow before tapping a few buttons on the control panel. He zoomed in on a shadowy figure making its way along one of the museum corridors. 'Exhibit A,' he said. 'There's our man!'

Lara felt a chill. *I've encountered him several times. I even have a bullet lodged in my side from an earlier meeting. And a bullet-holed ear!* She looked round at her pups and the children. *My priority is to keep you guys safe*, she thought. *But hang on . . .* Lara looked round the room again. She poked her head under the table. *Not there either.* Lara sniffed the air. *Even his smell is absent.* 'Where's Ollie?' she woofed to Star

and Spud. Lara's heart rate increased as she realized the youngest member of the Cook family was missing. His coat was abandoned on a chair. Lara picked it up and woofed for attention. The room fell silent and all eyes fell on the family pet. *Ollie's coat*, she thought, jabbing a paw. *But no Ollie. Anyone got any ideas?*

'That's Master Oliver's coat,' observed Professor Cortex. 'So what, GM451?'

It's not about the coat, thought Lara, jabbing her paw harder. *It's about the owner!*

'Where's Ollie?' said Sophie, scanning the room for her baby brother. The next five seconds of silence seemed an awful lot longer. All eyes followed Lara's gaze.

CCTV top row, third from left!

The sixth second brought a stifled gasp from Sophie. 'He's wandered off.' The grainy screen showed a black and white image of a little boy strolling through the Second World War exhibition. He was on a direct collision course with Mr Big.

12. Buying Time

'It's vitally important that nobody panics,' panicked Professor Cortex, reaching for his heart pills and struggling with the childproof cap. 'A clear mind is a sharp mind,' he stammered, pulling the cap off so hard that forty-five pills leapt from the tub and scattered across the room. 'Don't eat them!' he yelled, falling on to all fours and sweeping the pills up with his hand. 'Everything's under control.'

Lara looked around. She was the world's first-ever qualified Spy Dog. *Trained for missions. Primed for danger*, she thought. *But that was so long ago! If ever I needed to remember my training, it's now!*

Ben and Sophie were making for the door. Lara stood tall and blocked their escape. She held her paw out, ordering them to stop.

'We need to rescue Ollie,' gasped Sophie. 'What if he bumps into that evil man?'

'And it's all my fault,' wailed Ben. 'It was me who bugged your meeting and found out your plan.'

Was it indeed? thought Lara, shooing the children back into their seats. *We will rescue Ollie, but we need a plan.*

'What shall we do, Mum?' yapped Star.

Lara took a deep breath. *The professor's right about staying calm*, she thought as she watched him scuttling under a table in search of his pills. *He's already lost the plot. I have to keep Sophie and Ben safe. And we need to get to Ollie before he bumps into the ultimate bogeyman.* The retired Spy Dog glanced at the bank of CCTV screens again. Ollie was skipping along a dimly lit corridor. Mr Big was on screen 18, limping slowly and purposefully towards the Egyptian Room. Lara noticed he had a small computer in his hand. *Presumably he has the layout downloaded and is following a path. Think, Lara, think!*

'What shall we do, Mum?' yapped Star again impatiently. 'Ollie's on a collision course with someone you wouldn't want to bump into down a dark alley.'

Thanks for reminding me, thought Lara. 'Spud,' she barked. 'Log on to the central computer and find a floor plan of the building. Beam it on to the big screen so we can all see.'

'Already on it, Ma,' replied the puppy, tapping at a computer screen with a pencil, his tail wagging uncontrollably. 'We're here,' he said, jabbing at the screen. 'So we're quite near to the mummy. In fact, Ollie's nearly in the mummy room.'

'And Big's here,' woofed Star, her tongue lolloping in excitement. 'He's on the ground floor so has got to go up two flights of stairs. Why don't me and Spud go and delay him while you rescue Ollie?'

Professor Cortex was back on his feet, his face red after the exertion of crawling on the floor. He popped three pills into the palm of his hand and threw them into his mouth. 'GM451,' he began, 'I think I'd like to put you in charge of this mission.'

Lara raised an eyebrow. *Nice one, Prof*, she thought, nosing Ben's mobile phone towards the scientist. *Call for help, please*.

The man nodded vigorously. 'No need for that,' he frowned. 'Time to put titchology into practice.' Professor Cortex extended the thumb and little finger of his right hand. 'Nine nine nine,' he said, exaggerating the numbers so they were crystal clear. All eyes were on the professor as he waited. 'It's ringing,' he mouthed, pointing his left hand at the hand phone. 'Police, please. And, er, ambulance and fire brigade too, I think. And have you got anyone else? How about MI5? A helicopter would be nice. Have you got one of those yellow ones . . .?'

Lara's sticky-up ear stayed alert to the professor's phone call while the rest of her attention was devoted to the puppies. 'Good idea, Star,' she said. 'We have to delay Big from getting to the Egyptian Room.'

'I'd like to report a robbery at the British Museum,' explained the professor. 'The big one. In London. You know, the one that has pillars on the outside and it has a nice little cafe where you can buy flapjacks and Earl Grey. And the cheese toasties are rather yummy too, but you probably don't need to know that. It's all a little bit complicated so let me explain. We've broken in. Well, when I say "broken in", I don't really mean "broken in". We're not the problem, you see. It's not really us you need to arrest, although I do see how you might think breaking into the museum is actually a little big naughty. It's a bit sort of delicate . . .' jabbered the old man, his immense brain struggling in the heat of the moment.

Ben snatched at the professor's hand and held it to his own mouth. He felt dreadful for dragging his brother and sister into this adventure. 'Please send the emergency services at once,' he said calmly. 'There is a break-in involving the world's most evil criminal. He's going to steal a dead body. Oh, and if that isn't bad enough, there are children involved.' He glanced at the CCTV screen. 'One of them is very young. We're at the British Museum. We need help. And we need it now.'

Nice one, Ben, thought Lara. *That's how to stay cool under pressure!* 'Pups, go and delay Mr Big. The children and I will find Ollie. The police and ambulance are on their way. Meet you back here when the mission is complete.' *They know the drill, they'll be fine*, worried Lara, watching her pups getting into action mode.

Star was already out of the door. Spud was taking one last look at the computer screen, memorizing where Mr Big was. *It's a huge museum*, he thought. *On three floors. Direction is as important as speed*. 'Wait for me,' he yapped as he tore after his sister. 'We can cut him off at Ancient Greece.'

Mr Big was pleased with his progress. He'd visited the museum several times and done his homework. The two night guards had been easy to take out. He wasn't as quick on his feet as he used to be – not since his little 'accident'.

If falling from a plane could be described as an accident. 'That dog. And those awful kids,' he snarled, limping towards the Ancient Greece exhibition. 'They're the reason I've got a metal leg. And they're the ones I will track down and eliminate, just as soon as I've got my hands on the Nile Ruby.'

Star was waiting at the bottom of the stairs and her brother had positioned himself at the top. He was in the Chinese Room on the second floor. He'd had to be creative with weapons. The only things he could find in the China section were vases. *So many vases! I'm not sure who Ming was, but he sure churned out some pottery. Let's hope they won't miss a few old vases*, he thought as he lined them up. The puppy waited, chest heaving.

Mr Big came into view, limping heavily, his bionic knee joint squeaking. 'Needs oiling,' he muttered to himself as he approached the stairs. He was concentrating on following the map on his tablet computer. He didn't see a small dog peeping from behind a statue.

'Now,' woofed Star.

Mr Big was startled. He looked round in the direction of the barking. As he did so, an avalanche of vases cascaded over the balcony. The first clonked him on the head, sending him reeling. Two more shattered at his feet. He looked up and a Ming vase hit him full in the face, gashing his head. Mr Big was dazed. He wasn't sure what was going on, but he recognized a dog bark when he heard one. Nightmares rushed into his head.

Can't be, he thought, looking up towards the bombardment. He stepped back as another vase crashed over the balcony.

Mr Big had time on his side. If the stairs were blocked, he'd find another way into the Egyptian Room. He grabbed a sword from one of the exhibits. There was a saying running through his head about there being lots of ways to skin a cat. *But*, he thought, running his thumb along the edge of the blade, *that also applies to dogs*.

13. A Cunning Disguise

Lara tore through the museum corridors at top speed. 'Hiya, girl,' cooed Ollie as she careered round a corner. 'I've been doing a bit of exploring. This place is so cool!' he said, his eyes saucer-like with excitement. 'I've found a room full of ancient mummies!'

Ben and Sophie caught up and slid to a stop. 'We've been worried sick,' gasped Sophie. 'This is exactly where Mr Big is heading for.' The children and Lara looked round at the Egyptian exhibition. There were ancient artefacts everywhere. Jugs, cups, paintings and old scriptures. There were pictures of men with dogs' heads and plenty of pieces of sone. But the items that drew their attention most were the various mummified remains of Egyptian pharaohs.

Ollie approached a glass case and pointed at one. 'Why's he so small?'

'He's a child,' said Ben, reading the information. 'Akhtishu, the boy king. It says he died when he was eleven. And here he is, three thousand years later, in all his mummified glory.'

'And why are mummies men?' asked Ollie. 'Shouldn't they be called "daddies"?'

'It's creepy,' shivered Sophie. 'Glass cases full of dead bodies.'

Professor Cortex arrived on the scene, but was struggling to speak. He put his hands on his hips and sucked his cheeks in, swallowing lungfuls of air. 'Oliver! You're safe,' he wheezed at last, removing his glasses and dabbing his eyes. 'And, if the pups have delayed Big, we have a few minutes to make the mummy safe too,' he puffed. 'Here, Benjamin, help me find Qua'a. We can swap him for another mummy and Big will steal the wrong one. Genius idea or what?'

Lara stood guard while Ben and the professor got to work. Qua'a was lying in a wooden coffin, his arms crossed on his chest. There was no glass case so he was easy to get to. It was a delicate operation. Ben took the head end and the professor the feet. They lifted Qua'a out of his wooden coffin and lugged his bandaged body to another part of the exhibition. They laid him on a bench.

'Now what?' hissed Ben.

Lara started growling. 'That means Big's near,' panicked Ben. 'If he discovers the mummy is missing, there's no telling what he'll do!'

Lara's growls became more menacing. *Quick, guys*, she thought, *I can hear the sound of Big's metal foot clomping along the corridor.* The puppies had forced Mr Big to come the long way round, but he'd made it and here he was, face to face with the dog that had put him behind bars.

He stopped at the end of the corridor and gawped at Lara. 'Spy Dog!' He'd come to the museum to steal the world's most precious gem and he couldn't believe his luck. Now he could kill the dog too!

Sophie peered out of the Egyptian Room and squealed. 'It's him,' she squeaked. 'He's got a sword. I don't think Lara will be able to hold him off for very long.'

'OK, Benjamin,' said the professor. 'He's not after you or your brother or sister. I mean, he's evil and all that, but I doubt you're top of his list. I'd guess that he wants the ruby first and revenge on GM451 and myself second; after all, I made her into the superagent that she is! There's no way out except the way we came in. If Big catches me, I'm a goner,' gulped the professor. 'I need to hide.'

Ben was way ahead. He'd opened the first-aid kit that was hanging on the wall and was unwrapping the bandages. 'Five extra-large bandages,' he said. 'Professor, you will have to be the mummy.'

Ben got to work, starting at the professor's

feet and working his way up. Outside in the corridor Lara was buying them some time, barking her loudest barks and growling her fiercest growls. Her hackles were raised, teeth bared and adrenaline rushing through her veins. 'Two more minutes, Lara,' shrieked Sophie as her brother started on the fifth bandage.

Mr Big had stopped a few paces from Lara. *Why is he smiling?* she thought. *This is deadly serious and he's enjoying himself!*

Mr Big waved his sword in the air. 'Found it in the Roman section,' he said. 'Belonged to a famous gladiator who used it to slay his enemies.' He swished the sword again. 'So I thought it would be perfect.'

I'm no match for a man with a sword, thought Lara. She assessed the situation, the safety of the children at the forefront of her mind. *Spud and Star are yapping behind him and I'm guarding the entrance to the Egyptian Room*. Lara spied a fire-alarm button at the far end of the corridor. 'Hit it, Spud,' she barked. 'Let's make some noise.'

Spud jumped but couldn't reach. 'You do it, sis,' he yapped. 'It needs teamwork,' he added, crouching beneath the fire alarm. Star knew what to do. She sprinted at her brother, jumped on to his back and leapt into the air. She reached out and smashed her paw against the glass, a piercing alarm adding to the panic. Mr Big knew he didn't have long. The police would be arriving very soon. He decided to be bold. He stepped forward five paces. Lara held her ground, her lip curled and teeth bared. He swished the sword, cutting the air menacingly.

'Chop-chop, poochy,' he grinned.

Star couldn't contain her anger. She leapt at the man's ankle and tried to sink her teeth in. Mr Big calmly bent down and plucked the snarling puppy from his metal leg. 'Titanium, darling,' he smirked, dangling Star by her collar. Her legs were kicking, but her snarl was cut short by lack of oxygen. 'The harder you struggle, the more strangled you'll get.' Lara watched as Star kicked bravely. Spud sprinted to his mum, hiding close to her furry tummy.

'And now I have a hostage,' snarled the master-criminal. 'That gives me the upper hand. One false move, Spy Dog, and Scrappy Doo here gets it.' He dangled Star at arm's length. 'Got it?'

14. Off with his Head?

Lara's growling ceased. *I don't have much choice*, she thought, casting a glance at the professor and the children. Ben gave his dog the thumbs up and Lara backed off, allowing Mr Big into the Egyptian Room.

Professor Cortex was bandaged very tightly. His body lay in Qua'a's coffin, hardly breathing. Mr Big continued to hold Star at arm's length; her eyes were bulging and her kicking had stopped. He opened one of the glass cases and ushered the growling Lara and yapping Spud inside. He threw Star's limp body in after them and slid the door closed. He wedged the glass shut with a dagger and the barking was muffled. Star was sitting up, getting her breath back. Lara was barking fiercely and Spud was throwing himself at the glass, but it was no good.

Mr Big waved at the dogs. 'I'll deal with you later,' he yelled above the noise of the alarm. 'I have one more thing on my "to do" list,' he snarled, turning to the children.

Ben stood bravely to the fore, his sister and brother hiding behind him. 'Whaddaya want?' he asked.

'Some help,' said Mr Big, giving a politician's smile. 'We need to play "find a pharaoh". And the clock's ticking. If you and these meddling dogs have taken the trouble to find me, I'm guessing you know which mummy I'm after?'

'Qua'a,' blurted Ben. 'Because you know about the legend of the Nile Ruby.'

'I know the *truth* of the Nile Ruby,' purred Mr Big, walking through the exhibition, peering at the information above each mummy. He stopped at the bandaged professor, his eyes shining. 'Qua'a!' he exclaimed. 'You're everything I'd hoped for.' He bent down and touched Ben's hastily wrapped bandages. 'You've aged so well.' He looked up at the children, who were hardly daring to breathe. 'Where are the adults?' he snarled. 'Mum and Dad?'

'It's just us,' said Ben, sweeping his arm round the room. 'Lara knew you'd be here. I guess she wanted a final showdown. We just followed her. There are no adults.'

'What about that nutty professor?'

'He's a mummy . . .' began Ollie.

'His mummy,' interrupted Ben, 'is poorly. So he's looking after her,' he said, nudging his little brother in the ribs.

Mr Big knew he didn't have time for any more questions. The emergency services had arrived and he could hear distant shouting above the sound of the piercing alarm. He eyed the gladiator's sword and then the mummy. 'I don't need the whole thing,' he snarled. 'The gem's in the head. I just need the head!'

Ben could have sworn he heard the mummy gulp. He thought quickly. 'I've got an idea,' he said, calm on the outside, heart pounding in his eardrums. 'I can help you escape. But you're going to need the whole mummy. The best plans are always simple, right? This place will be swarming with paramedics. So we lay the prof . . . *pharaoh* . . . Qua'a . . . on a stretcher and walk out of the front door.'

Lara had calmed Spud and they watched the silent action from behind the glass. Her sharp eyes saw the mummy's chest collapse with relief as the baddie laid his sword on the floor. Mr Big grabbed Sophie by the scruff of the neck and approached the glass cabinet. He waved his sword towards the dogs. 'Sit,' he ordered. 'And shut up!' He opened the glass case and bundled Sophie and Ollie into the display. Mr Big slid the door shut and rammed the dagger in place, sealing them in, in silent terror.

'Here, you grab his legs.' Mr Big and Ben heaved the bandaged scientist from the display. 'Crikey, the old pharaoh's a lot heavier than I expected,' said the baddie. 'Here, stick him on this Egyptian rug and we'll use it as a stretcher.' Sophie and Ollie watched in disbelief as the professor was rolled on to a rug. Mr Big started dragging the rug out of the room. 'Come on, boy,' he yelled, 'get a grip!'

The professor's bandaged frame was hauled along the museum's polished floor. They reached the lift and Mr Big jabbed impatiently at the button. 'Come on, come on,' he muttered as the doors pinged open and they dragged the mummy inside.

Mr Big eyed Ben as the lift descended. 'I'll do the talking,' he warned. 'You play along . . . or else,' he said, running his finger across his throat.

'Ground floor,' announced the lift. 'Doors opening.' The silver doors parted and Ben and Mr Big stood either side of the mummified professor. The professor couldn't see a thing, but he could hear the commotion. The fire alarm had finally been switched off and the museum entrance was swarming with the emergency services. Police were running here and there. The fire brigade were mob-handed.

'Over here!' yelled Mr Big to a paramedic in a green outfit. 'Injured man. Get me a stretcher.' While the chaos continued, Professor Cortex was loaded on to a stretcher and carried to an ambulance.

'Looks bad,' said the medic. 'What happened to him?'

'Fire,' blurted Ben, looking terrified as he remembered the finger across the throat.

'Fell down the stairs,' said Mr Big at the same time. 'Er, there was a fire and then he sort of fell down the stairs,' he said, glaring at Ben.

'Sounds like he's had some bad luck. Let's get the poor fella into the ambulance and we'll check him out on the way to the hospital.' The professor was loaded aboard. The medic had trained to be one because he was a good man: trusting, kind and helpful.

'There's a kid too,' snarled Mr Big. 'Third floor. He needs urgent assistance. I'll wait with this one while you fetch the poor little wounded orphan,' he said, overacting terribly.

The medic nodded and was off, sprinting

back into the museum on a wild goose chase. Mr Big was delighted that the driver only required one punch. It was a matter of seconds before he'd secured Ben and the mummy in the back of the ambulance and himself in the front seat. He checked the controls, hit the siren button and screeched the vehicle on to London's night streets.

15. A Very Slow Getaway

Terror Thomas sat bolt upright in bed. His hair was as wild as his temper. Who on earth was ringing him at 2 a.m.? He fumbled for the light switch and his good eye blinked in the light. He put his mobile to his ear. 'Yes?' he barked. 'This had better be good.'

He listened intently. His second-in-command was jabbering about the fire alarm going off and the police arriving. 'It's not a fire. It's intruders, sir,' he said. 'We think they've taken out the security team. They've smashed a load of priceless Ming vases and it seems likely that they've made off with one of the Egyptian mummies.'

Terror Thomas didn't need any more information. He'd spent fifteen years at the sharp end of the army, on duty in the desert. It had been a career full of action, fighting, suspense and thrills. He'd lost his eye along the way and now his days were spent watching teenagers from the corner of his good eye or glaring at small children to make sure they didn't steal sweets from the museum shop. His life was dull, dull and dull. And here he was, plunged into a *real* emergency. He put the phone on speaker so he could get dressed while he listened to the pandemonium. His pyjama trousers were off and one leg was in his pants before he realized both his feet were rammed into one hole. 'Curses, curses,' he said, having a second go. *Having one eye can sometimes be a real bummer.*

'And what's happening now,' he yelled, buttoning his shirt.

'Ambulances have just turned up,' yelled his assistant above the noise of a helicopter. 'And the bomb squad. This is big, sir. Code red. Please hurry.'

Thomas looked in the bedroom mirror. *Code red! How awesome!* He'd got dressed in less than a minute so looked a bit of a mess. But it was the early hours of the morning – looking good was a luxury he didn't have time for. He reached for his wallet and tucked it into his back pocket. 'Just got to put my eye in,' he shouted to the man on the other end of the phone. 'And I'll be right with you.'

Terror Thomas's fingers swished in the water, feeling for his glass eye. His thumb and fore-finger settled on Spud's pickled onion and he shook the water away before ramming it into his eye socket.

The man on the other end of the phone nearly jumped out of his skin. He had never heard a yell quite as loud or quite as long.

It took a while for the police to understand what Sophie and Ollie were on about. The little boy was so excited that everything came out in one long sentence. 'The professor is a mummy and he got taken away by a baddie and Lara, our pet Spy Dog, well, she's retired now so isn't actually a spy, but she is a dog, tried to save everyone and we really need our real mummy . . .'

'Yes, yes,' soothed the lady police officer. She was trained to remain calm and the children were obviously in shock. Sophie and Ollie were wrapped in foil blankets and led down the stairs, Ollie complaining that he felt like a roast chicken.

Star had made a good recovery and was

doubly determined to recapture the evil Mr Big. Lara and the pups ran ahead, looking out for Ben. Lara led, head and tail down, taking the slippery floor at full speed. She careered through the main door and out into the night air. A paramedic was standing at the entrance, scratching his head. 'Where's my ambulance gone?' he said. 'And my bandaged patient?'

Lara was in Spy Dog mode, fitting the clues together in her head. *Stolen ambulance. Man in bandages. I need to find that vehicle.* She assessed the situation. There were people milling about, but nobody seemed to be in charge. Lara remembered her training. *Then I must take charge*, she thought, taking a deep breath and puffing out her chest.

She watched as Sophie and Ollie were led to a police car. A policewoman opened the back door and ushered them in. *An opportunity*, thought the dog as the officer walked away. Lara and the pups jumped aboard. The retired Spy Dog took Sophie's phone and logged on to the Internet. There was a minute of silence except for some serious tapping of paw on screen. 'Gotcha,' woofed Lara, holding the map out to the puppies. 'That dot is the professor's phone. The one implanted in his hand. His titchology thing.'

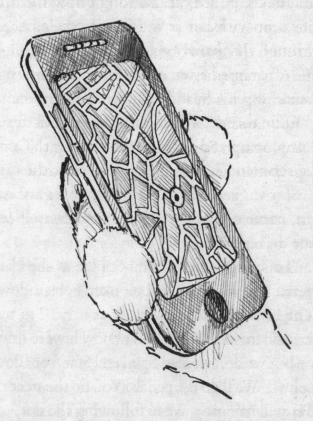

'So we need to follow that dot,' yapped Star. 'Before Mr Big discovers that the mummy isn't really a mummy,' added Spud. 'And the prof . . . you know . . .' he woofed, running his paw across his throat.

'Before the professor loses his head,' agreed

Lara. 'We've no time to lose.' Sophie looked a little unsure as Lara jumped into the passenger seat of the police car. The dog patted the driver's seat with her paw. 'Come on, lady,' she whined. *We haven't got all day. Your brother has been kidnapped by an evil baddie. And you've got hands, so you have to do the steering.*

Ollie threw off his foil wrapper and started jumping up and down in the back seat. 'Cool!' he shouted. 'Lara wants you to steer the car.'

Star tugged at Sophie's trouser leg. 'Come on, come on,' she snarled. 'Get yourself into the driver's seat.'

'This is ridiculous,' said Sophie as she clambered into the front and plonked herself down. The little girl looked sternly at Lara. 'I'm ten,' she said frostily. 'And I don't know how to drive.'

'But we do,' woofed Spud and Star from down below. 'We'll do the pedals. You do the steering. Ma will navigate. We're following the dot.'

'That's the plan,' woofed the family pet. 'Pups, give me some revs and away we go. The car is an automatic so we only have two pedals.'

Sophie looked down at her feet.

'"Stop" – that's me,' waved Star.

'And guess who's in charge of "Go"?' grinned

Spud, sitting his heavy bottom on the pedal and revving the police car.

Lara slammed the lever into 'Drive' mode and pressed a button to release the handbrake. The police car bumped onward and Star fell on to the brake, screeching the car to an emergency stop. Everyone lurched forward. 'Strap yourself in, Ollie,' warned Sophie. 'This could get hairy.'

Spud revved the accelerator pedal again and Star shifted off the brake. 'Not too fast, pups,' warned Lara from the passenger seat. 'Sophie has got to get the hang of steering.'

A policeman noticed his car kangarooing along the road and started running. He caught up with the driver's window and peered in at a girl driver wrapped in foil. He knocked loudly and they heard a muffled voice: 'Stop, thief!'

Sophie knew that if she stopped she'd have to spend an hour explaining the situation. And, if they wanted the professor's head to remain attached to his shoulders, that was an hour they didn't have. 'This could be life or death. Hit it, Spud,' she said, and the puppy slammed his weighty bottom on to the accelerator. Sophie

smiled weakly at the policeman as his car accelerated away.

Terror Thomas was in the thick of it.

He'd thrown himself around his bedroom
while the vinegar had seeped into his eye
socket. Try as he might, he couldn't get the
pickle out, but the pain had subsided and he
knew there was no time to lose.

So he'd pulled up at the museum with one

good eye and one with a pickled onion rammed into the socket. He looked in the rear-view mirror, his veggie eye puffy and red. The head of security had arrived in the nick of time. It was chaotic. His good eye had blinked in amazement as he watched a man and a boy load a bandaged body into the back of an ambulance before driving off. And his pickled onion eye had watered with astonishment as a couple of kids and three dogs had taken off in a stolen police car.

Terror Thomas was ex-army. He knew he needed to keep a clear head and think things through. The police were busy sealing off the area. There were six fire engines and a bomb-squad van. Emergency service staff were hurrying to and fro, but nobody seemed to know what was going on. Everything was just a little odd. But the oddest things of all were a stolen ambulance and police car.

He weighed things up in his mind. *I can stay and join in with the chaos. Or . . .* He let the handbrake off and revved his engine in pursuit of Sophie's police car.

16. A HAPI Ending

Mr Big had used his ambulance siren to clear what traffic there was. He and Ben had made good progress. 'If it was a road-sweeping lorry, I'd call it a "clean getaway". But it's an ambulance so I'll call it a "clinical getaway",' he smirked.

Ben didn't laugh.

'It was a great idea, lad,' smiled Mr Big. 'Stealing the whole mummy. I'll extract the ruby from its head and maybe sell the mummy to a dealer. Might make some extra cash. You, young man, have the makings of an excellent criminal mind.'

The ambulance reached the outskirts of London and Mr Big calmed the siren. He pulled up outside a warehouse and yanked the handbrake on. 'I need your help to drag the mummy inside,' he said, holding Ben by the scuff of his neck. 'No funny biz, OK? Or I'll track down your dogs and all three of them will get it.'

Ben gulped. He wasn't sure what 'it' was, but it didn't sound remotely funny. The boy followed the baddie to the back of the ambulance and the doors were yanked open. The mummified professor lay on a stretcher. 'Let's get this old boy inside,' snarled the man.

Ben was picturing the professor's reaction to the 'old boy' comment as he helped march the stretcher into the deserted warehouse. Mr Big had clearly been here before. He carried the front of the stretcher, Ben following. 'In here,' said Mr Big, pushing open a door with his foot.

Ben was relieved to slide the professor on to a kitchen table. 'He's quite a weight, this mummy,' said the boy, shaking his arms and hands to ease the pain.

'That'll be the weight of the Nile Ruby,' grinned the baddie. 'It's the biggest and therefore the heaviest gem in the entire world.' He reached over and slid open a drawer. He pulled out a kitchen knife and held it up to the light. Ben and the mummy gulped as the blade shone in the light. 'And soon,' laughed Mr Big, 'that ruby will be mine!'

★

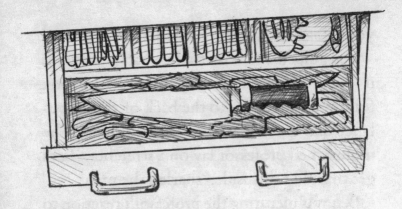

Sophie was struggling to see out of the windscreen. Luckily the little girl was only in charge of steering. Lara was sitting in the passenger seat, her neck strained, barking instructions to the pups and indicating left or right with her paws. The Spy Pups couldn't see anything. They were at Sophie's feet. Spud was the acceleration and Star the brake.

To the citizens of London who were going about their night-time business, this was anything but a high-speed chase. Lara was barking very careful instructions and the police car was cruising slowly through the streets, occasionally juddering to a halt. Sophie's knuckles were as white as her face and the pups could hear her squeaking in alarm. 'A corner,' she said. 'What do I do?'

I wish I could speak, thought Lara. *This is one*

of those moments when I could offer a calm and relaxed perspective. 'Just turn the wheel and the car will follow,' I'd say. 'That's right. Feed the steering wheel through your hands . . .'

Sophie panicked and turned the car too sharply. *There goes a wing mirror*, noted Lara. 'Straight bit, Spud, hit the pedal.'

The police car accelerated. Sophie screamed. 'I don't like this,' she wailed. 'I'm too young to drive. And especially to die.'

Nobody's going to die, thought Lara. *At least not if we can find Ben and the professor in time*. She jabbed a paw at a few buttons and the map refreshed. *They've pulled up at a warehouse three miles north of here*.

'Star,' she barked, 'take a break. Spud . . . hit it!'

Ben had done the best wrapping he could, but there were some loose ends. The bandage around the professor's head was beginning to come loose and he was pretty sure that if you looked closely enough one of the professor's ears was poking through.

'Hang on a second, Big,' said Ben bravely. 'There's no need for knives.'

Mr Big was thinking things through. Ben's brain was working equally rapidly. He knew Lara would be able to track the professor's mobile device and would know his whereabouts. He needed to stall for time. 'You want the Nile Ruby, right?'

The criminal nodded, a strange sound of satisfaction and desperation vibrating in his throat. 'It's in that mummy's head. So I figure that the quickest way of getting at it is simply to remove the head. Let's face it, it's not something that I haven't done before,' he purred.

Ben felt for the HAPI crystals in his pocket. He couldn't see that there was anything amusing in this situation, but it was his only chance. 'But this mummy is three thousand years old,' he argued. 'You can't just slice its head off!'

'Wanna bet?' smiled Mr Big, taking a step towards the body.

Professor Cortex had had enough. He was trussed very tightly and couldn't talk. But he could hear. 'That's it,' he mumbled. 'I'm calling the police.' He couldn't move his joints, but managed to rock himself into an upright position.

Mr Big dropped the knife as the mummy sat up. Ben took the bag of HAPI crystals in his fingers and sprinkled them on to the floor. He ground his shoe into them and a strange smell wafted through the room.

Sophie had done remarkably well. If it was an official driving test, she would have failed on 'failing to stop at a zebra crossing' (twice), 'failing to stop at a red light' (twice), 'losing both wing mirrors', 'mounting the kerb' (several times), 'going the wrong way down a one-way street' and 'failing to look in the rear-view mirror'. So, as her stolen police car juddered to a stop next to the ambulance, she failed to notice Terror Thomas pulling up twenty metres behind. He switched off his lights and watched as a big dog, two puppies and a girl and boy entered a deserted warehouse.

Lara's priority was always the welfare of the children. It had been drilled into her: *Rule number one, look after the children. Keep them from harm. There are no other rules*. So she'd left Sophie and Ollie in the safety of the warehouse. *Stay*, she ordered, putting her paw up to show she was serious. *You guys do not move from this room until I come and get you*.

Lara and the puppies left the room. All were in Spy Dog mode, primed and ready for action. There was light coming from under the kitchen door and a huge commotion from within. The pups perched on Lara's shoulders and she stood tall, peering through the kitchen window.

Lara had seen active service on missions around the world. She'd battled with evil villains and had adventures that made her fur stand on end. But she'd never seen anything quite like this.

'It's alive!' stammered the criminal as Professor Cortex sat up and waved his arms around.

'Get these bandages off me, Benjamin,' he yelled, although to Mr Big it sounded like the muffled sound of a mummy's curse.

Ben took advantage of the criminal's shock and ran to the professor. He started at the top of his body, unwinding the bandages, revealing a bald head and then a very purple face. 'Thank goodness for that,' spat the professor. 'Crikey, it was hot in there, Benjamin.' The professor seemed more angry than scared. He jabbed a bandaged hand at his bald head. 'There is no Nile Ruby in here,' he yelled at Mr Big. 'Just the world's finest scientific brain. And it does *not* want to be removed from its head.'

'It's him,' sniggered Mr Big. 'The mad professor,' he said, cupping his hand to his mouth to stifle an even bigger laugh.

'Yes,' huffed the professor. 'It most certainly is me,' he chuckled. 'And, quite frankly, sir, the last thing I want is you . . . you know,' he sniggered, 'removing my head.'

The HAPI gas was working its magic. 'But I'm going to kill you,' giggled Mr Big, reaching for a bigger knife.

Ben had already sunk to his knees. 'He thought you were a mummy,' he wheezed, pointing at the world's most evil criminal. 'He's going to kill you,' laughed the boy, his eyes streaming. 'By hacking your head off.'

'I am,' howled Mr Big, gripping the handle of the knife. 'Both of you . . .' he laughed, one hand clutching his side. 'Starting with the old chap.'

Lara wasn't sure what to do. Sophie and Ollie were safe, at least for the time being. She continued to peer through the window and watched Ben fall to his knees, disabled with laughter. *Think, Lara, think*.

Just then Terror Thomas came careering down the passageway. He saw the dogs peering through the window. He burst through the kitchen door just as Mr Big was staggering towards the bandaged Professor Cortex. Everyone stopped. Heads turned to see who had come in. Terror Thomas sniffed the air. 'What's that strange smell?' he smiled.

'Look at his eye,' howled Professor Cortex. 'He's got a pickled eye! He's gone and inserted one of Spud's pickled onions . . .'

Mr Big was laughing so hard it hurt. There was a clink as his knife hit the floor. Ben took his chance and manoeuvred the professor off the table.

'He's got a pickled onion for an eye,' howled

Mr Big. 'And who's Spud? That's the funniest name I've ever heard.'

'It's not funny actually,' chuckled Terror Thomas, the HAPI gas working its way into his bloodstream. He pointed to his eye. 'It's actually very painful,' he howled. 'And . . .' he laughed, his sides beginning to ache, '. . . it's stuck.'

Ben and the professor's eyes were streaming with tears. Ben pointed at Mr Big's trousers. 'There's a wet patch,' he yelped, his body aching with laughter. 'He's let out a bit of wee.' Ben was bent double with laughter. 'The world's most evil criminal has wet his pants.'

Mr Big looked down at his trousers, his eyes gaping, his mouth sucking in air. 'I have,' he howled, pointing at the wet patch. 'And it's going to be even funnier when I murder you both.' His hand yanked at the cutlery drawer and he fumbled for the first thing he could find. 'With a fork!' he bellowed, brandishing his new weapon.

Ben and the men crawled on the floor for a few moments, wracked with laughter at the thought of killing someone with a fork. Ben watched as Mr Big and Terror Thomas clambered upright, tears streaming. Thomas threw a punch. Mr Big ducked and Thomas spun round, falling to the floor. Mr Big was helpless with laughter ('. . . *a pickled onion* . . .') as Thomas rose to his feet once more. The evil baddie ran at Thomas with a cross between a blood-curdling scream and a yelp for help. He'd completely lost control of his bladder. He staggered across the room, fork outstretched. Terror Thomas ducked, but there was contact and the fork sank into his pickled onion eye.

Lara and the puppies winced from behind the glass. *That's gonna hurt*, thought Lara as Terror Thomas staggered round the kitchen, trying to pull it out.

The laughter stopped for a second and there was a squelching sound and the security guard held the fork aloft. The pickled onion eye wiggled on the end of the fork and that was it. 'It's out!'

Mr Big and Terror Thomas sank to the floor in hysterics.

'Eye eye,' gasped Mr Big as a muscle pulled in his stomach.

'I'll keep my eye out for you,' wheezed Thomas, crawling on his hands and knees.

Lara took her chance. She held her breath and rammed open the door. She dragged Ben out first, tugging him by the jeans. 'Get him outside,' she barked to the pups. 'He needs fresh air. Lots of it.'

The retired Spy Dog held her breath once more and went back in. The professor was bent double by the sink, laughing so hard that he could hardly breathe. 'He had a pickled onion eye . . .' Terror Thomas and Mr Big were helpless on the floor.

'Come on, old man,' she woofed. Lara stood on her hind legs and grabbed the professor by a bandaged arm and dragged him out of the kitchen. There was a satisfying click as she locked the kitchen door.

17. An Even Happier Ending

'And that was pretty much that,' said the professor gravely, avoiding eye contact with Mrs Cook.

'You seem to be portraying yourself as some sort of hero, Professor,' nagged Mrs Cook, the veins sticking out in her forehead.

The dogs knew she was approaching boiling point. Lara and Star lowered their ears and sank their bellies towards the floor. Spud's was already there.

'Well, I did nearly lose my head . . .' began the professor.

'As far as I'm concerned, I wish you had,' yelled Mum. 'You somehow managed to drag my children into a museum . . .'

'At midnight,' added Ollie unhelpfully.

'At midnight. In London. With an evil man

who's intent on doing harm to my children.'

'Don't forget stealing the car,' added Ollie as Ben aimed a kick at his little brother.

'Look, Mum,' began Ben. 'It was me who got us involved. The prof was dead against it . . .'

The door opened and a sharp-suited man appeared. 'The Prime Minister will see you now,' he smiled as the mood calmed and the Cook family and their dogs filed in.

The Prime Minister was standing tall and proud. He welcomed each member of the family with a warm smile and a firm handshake. 'Welcome, welcome,' he enthused. 'And please make yourselves comfortable. My government, indeed this country, owes you a big debt.'

Spud had already spied the trolley. While everyone else headed for the comfy leather chairs, the rotund puppy leapt on to the trolley and slid some food on to a plate. *This is all the thanks I need*, he thought. 'Here,' he woofed, 'Star, check this out.' His sister looked up. Spud had created a face with pickled onion eyes, cheese nose and hammy smile.

'Looks like old Terror Thomas,' sniggered his sister. 'The eyes are perfect!'

Everyone else's eyes were fixed on the Prime Minister, who was in serious mode. 'Obviously,' he soothed, looking at Mrs Cook, 'we never intended for the children to get involved.'

'We didn't mind,' chirped Ollie. 'We like missions. And have you got any fizzy drinks?'

'But the fact is that they did get involved,' continued the PM. 'And played an active part in recapturing the evil Mr Big. It's no exaggeration to say that the streets are much safer this evening with that man locked in solitary confinement.'

Lara looked at Mum. *She seems calmer. The PM is very good!*

'So,' continued the Prime Minister, 'I think your dogs and children should be rewarded.'

'Rewarded?' smiled Mrs Cook, stretching her neck with pride. Tails wagged and the children sat up straight.

'It seems Dr Desmond Farquhar had quite a history,' said the PM, glancing down at some notes. 'And do you know what? I don't think he was actually a bad man. More a *tormented* man.'

Professor Cortex took up the story. 'Qua'a's resting place was a huge find. But the good doc wasn't a tomb robber at all. It was only the Nile

Ruby that he really wanted. Most adventurers of that era would have plundered the cave and stolen whatever they could. But not Dr Farquhar. He tried to reseal Qua'a's resting place and keep it hidden. But, sadly, the secret was out and other people helped themselves. Qua'a himself was brought to his final resting place, the British Museum.'

'It's a great story, Prof,' smiled Sophie. 'But why did he get sent to prison?'

'Well,' continued the professor, 'Farquhar returned from Egypt, pretty much a celebrity of his day. Did lots of guest lectures, wrote a couple of books, met the Queen. That kind of thing . . .'

'And then it dawned on him,' said the PM, unable to resist such an exciting tale, 'that the book had been right in every detail. That the Nile Ruby had indeed been buried *inside* the coffin. And this is the gruesome bit,' he said, casting a warning eye at Mum. 'It seems that during the mummification process, Qua'a's brain had been removed and replaced with his most precious possession . . .'

'The ruby!' gasped Ollie. 'It really was in his head!'

'Bingo!' nodded the professor. 'We had Qua'a X-rayed and, sure enough, there's a precious stone inside his head.' He handed round a black and white X-ray which, one by one, everyone held towards the light.

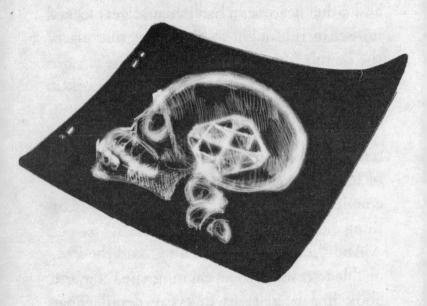

That's a huge gem, marvelled Lara. *Must be worth a fortune.*

'One hundred carats,' noted the professor, Spud's ears pricking up at the sound of food. 'And it's going to remain a secret,' he warned. 'But you can see why the good doctor felt he had to act on his father's dying wish and get his mitts on the ruby. He didn't intend to sell it. He was only interested in telling the world that his dad was a hero. Hence breaking and entering thirty-four times, the final one of which resulted in an unfortunate accident involving a security guard and, hey presto, the good doc becomes a bad doc and gets locked up in Hurtmore.'

'Which is exactly where Mr Big is right now,' said the Prime Minister, grinning his biggest grin of the day. 'The judge upped his stay in prison to *eighteen* life sentences. So a few rewards are in order, don't you think?'

Spud was coaxed down from the trolley and the dogs were lined up. A woman in a cloak appeared with a cushion. 'Medals!' gasped Mum.

The PM bent down and attached a medal round the neck of each dog. Lara stretched her neck proudly. Star almost fainted with excitement. Spud cast an eye back at the trolley.

'For going way beyond the call of duty,' said the PM. There was a small round of applause for the dogs. 'And something for your very brave and courageous children,' he smiled. 'Professor Cortex, I think you have something special for them?'

There was an awkward moment as the professor rummaged in his pockets. 'I certainly do,' he said, pulling out some sachets of milk-shake powder. 'A world-first in fact. Rhubarb & mustard for you,' he beamed, handing a sachet to Ben.

'Spag Bol for you,' he said, thrusting a packet at Ollie.

Sophie retched at the thought of savoury milkshake. 'And, for you,' he said, reserving his biggest grin for the little girl, 'I've developed . . . *frogs' leg surprise!*'

Sophie's hand went to her mouth and the colour left her cheeks. 'The *surprise* being that it's otherwise known as . . . *raspberry ripple*,' he assured her. 'My little joke.'

Lara was enjoying her own little joke.

Terror Thomas had been delighted to take up the offer of a new job. Especially one that involved the potential for danger and excite-ment. Head of the solitary confinement wing at Hurtmore Prison was perfect. As the new governor had explained at the interview, 'You can keep your eye on Big.'

Lara knew the professional criminal would

be in solitary so had decided he needed cheering up. A grin spread across Terror Thomas's face as he unwrapped the small package and read the letter. 'Ultra-strength HAPI crystals. Just sprinkle into his cell and run.' Thomas adjusted his eyepatch and straightened his tie. He was really looking forward to going to work.

As the children and dogs were receiving their awards, Mr Big was laughing so hard it hurt. Lara's arch-enemy was on his hands and knees, wheezing in pain. Three stomach muscles had popped, his eyes were watering and his pants were sodden. 'Spy Dog has caused this,' he gasped, struggling to suck in enough breath. 'I'm going to get that dratted mutt,' he howled as he hammered the floor, another muscle twanging under the pressure.

The evil baddie's face was as red as the Nile Ruby. 'This place can't hold me. Eighteen life sentences . . . that's the funniest thing I've ever heard!'

Bright and shiny and sizzling with fun stuff . . .

puffin.co.uk

WEB FUN

UNIQUE and exclusive digital content!
Podcasts, photos, Q&A, Day in the Life of, interviews
and much more, from Eoin Colfer, Cathy Cassidy,
Allan Ahlberg and Meg Rosoff to Lynley Dodd!

WEB NEWS

The **Puffin Blog** is packed with posts and photos from
Puffin HQ and special guest bloggers. You can also sign up
to our monthly newsletter **Puffin Beak Speak**

WEB CHAT

Discover something new EVERY month –
books, competitions and treats galore

WEBBED FEET

(Puffins have funny little feet and
brightly coloured beaks)

Point your mouse our way today!

It all started with a Scarecrow

Puffin is over seventy years old.
Sounds ancient, doesn't it? But Puffin has never been
so lively. We're always on the lookout for the next big
idea, which is how it began all those years ago.

Penguin Books was a big idea from the mind of
a man called Allen Lane, who in 1935 invented
the quality paperback and changed the world.
**And from great Penguins, great Puffins grew,
changing the face of children's books forever.**

The first four Puffin Picture Books were hatched in 1940 and the
first Puffin story book featured a man with broomstick arms called
Worzel Gummidge. In 1967 Kaye Webb, Puffin Editor, started the
Puffin Club, promising to **'make children into readers'**.
She kept that promise and over 200,000 children became devoted
Puffineers through their quarterly instalments of *Puffin Post*.

Many years from now, we hope you'll look back and
remember Puffin with a smile. **No matter what your age
or what you're into, there's a Puffin for everyone.**
The possibilities are endless, but one thing is for sure:
whether it's a picture book or a paperback, a sticker book
or a hardback, **if it's got that little Puffin
on it – it's bound to be good.**